Two Roses

Mazen Kharboutli

authorHOUSE®

AuthorHouse™ UK
1663 Liberty Drive
Bloomington, IN 47403 USA
www.authorhouse.co.uk
Phone: 0800.197.4150

Published by AuthorHouse   06/26/2018

ISBN: 978-1-5462-9365-1 (sc)
ISBN: 978-1-5462-9364-4 (hc)
ISBN: 978-1-5462-9369-9 (e)

To my cherished family and others who provided the inspiration and encouragement to manifest this writing, I extend heartfelt thanks. Never could I have fulfilled my goal without you.

Foreword

If you don't see the light at the end of the tunnel,
light up your side, and someone will notice.

—Mazen Kharboutli

The past can be an albatross—a huge, obstructive creature that coils around your neck and doesn't let go. At intervals, the past can also manifest as a sorcerer, luring you into believing that you are inextricably bound by its commands, divested of free will. It mercilessly flashes painful memories, images, words, and sounds that echo interminably in the recesses of your mind, consuming and preventing you from moving forward toward the light in the proverbial tunnel. But what if there is no light in sight, and you are utterly, helplessly directionless?

Such was the case with Daniel Bouchard, a boy stuck in the time tunnel of yesterday, hearing nothing but the echoes of his lonely heart. Dwelling in a mecca of material abundance, he nonetheless felt alone, forgotten, and marginalized. Most of all, he felt unloved, yearning to find the definition of that sacred four-letter word and its unmitigated expression: *love".*"

In the earliest days of his childhood, Daniel's mother succumbed to a terminal illness, robbing her of her rightful role as mother and caregiver, leaving her bereaved husband to single-handedly raise their four young children.

Then, the unthinkable happened. Fate caught Daniel and his siblings in its cruel clutches once again when the family experienced another unexpected, devastating loss. All at once, the children's world was enshrouded in the depths of darkness. Every joy and comfort they had ever known vanished in an instant, replaced with uncertainty, sorrow, and an overwhelming feeling of love starvation. For a while, they held on to the apron strings of their grandmother, who was everything to them, but even in the presence of her all-encompassing care and nurturing, she could not possibly resurrect their former sense of security.

Other than clinging to one another as they tried to make ends meet, Daniel had the burning desire to leave the past behind and rediscover himself in a new land. There was only one glaring problem: the spirit of the forlorn orphan came with him, infused with pain, loss, and indecisiveness. All the while, he kept his heart under lock and key. Essentially, he wanted to escape his enormous unrest but failed to embrace the lessons that the past was trying to teach him.

As he grew, Daniel's gaping emotional wounds threatened to destroy him, and he made decisions of which he wasn't proud. He realized, however, that to err is human, and he muddled through, always looking for "that special someone" who would fulfill every need and facet of his life. In so doing, he learned that love of that magnitude can lift you to the heights of exaltation and then, all at once, drag you into the depths of despair.

Daniel emerged from his first-love experience with the still unanswerable question: "Who am I?" He had no one to turn to for the answer—no one, that is, but the boy he left behind, whose heart and spirit still lived within him, the cause of his tears and disappointments and his misplaced tendency to seek the attributes of a loving heart in one person alone. That decision proved to be a tragic flaw, but he was left with the possibility of redemption—if he only could make the right choices.

Although Daniel is a fictitious character, he is intended to be every man—indeed, every person—who is searching for love, light, and belonging. Which one of us Earth pilgrims can genuinely say that we are immune to these feelings? The foibles of humanity lie in everyone, and the journey is a vast, frightening search through the tunnel of life. Sometimes, there is desperation in the thought of not finding what you seek. However, if you truly listen, there is supreme joy in the knowledge that home is not that far away—if you light your side of the tunnel and move in the direction of your heart, guided by the compass within.

—Mazen Kharboutli

Introduction

The path to love is paved with joy and pain, by turns. As the saying goes, "if you love something, let it go. If it was meant to be yours, it will return to you. If not, it was never meant to be." Daniel Bouchard had to let go many times in his life. Cruel circumstance seems to have dictated the course of his destiny, and he harbored a deep-seated sense of loss. In every phase of his life, original grief—a kind of foundational mourning that developed since his early childhood—surfaced within him and manifested in various ways, particularly in his ability to sustain and cultivate relationships and commitments.

In order to find love, therefore, Daniel had to dig deep within and encounter himself. He had to evolve and mature by admitting mistakes, assuming personal accountability, and rectifying his missteps. He also had to face the fact that everything that happened to him was not necessarily *about* him at all. There were other lives affected by his actions—his offhanded treatment of the women whose hearts he had captured, as well as some very wrong decisions that had emotionally dire outcomes. Virtually everything that occurred to and around him was the result of abandonment issues, hurt, and grief, all of which he had to face with a heart and mind wide open, ready to receive the pain and reap the rewards of growth.

For all those who have loved and lost, Daniel wants you to know that there is a sun that rises over a new day with brand-new possibilities—if only you have the courage to face that which holds you back. Life is precious in all of its facets, and it is there for us to claim, but this must be done with self-introspection, ensuing self-awareness, and a willingness to reach beyond the ego to encounter something *far greater* than the self—the capacity to love unconditionally, accept the ones you love as they are instead of what they could be, and know that love is the ultimate answer.

Chapter 1

A Pit of Loneliness

Daniel Bouchard lived in the enchanted city of Paris, France. When he looked out of his window, he beheld the Avenue des Champs-Élysées, one of the most beautiful boulevards in the world, with its boutique shops and restaurants filled with bustling activity all year round. He especially enjoyed Christmastime, when the bright lights of the city seemed to illuminate the universe as far as the eye could see.

If anyone peered into Daniel's world, they would think that he and his older siblings, Marie, Collette, and Pierre, lived charmed lives, and by all appearances, that was the case. Yet, something was missing—not *something* exactly, but rather *someone*. Tragically, his young mother, Michelle, had passed away after a battle with cancer at age thirty-three, leaving the family behind to navigate the world without her while emotionally dealing with their incomprehensible loss.

The children—and Daniel, in particular—always grappled with the absence of a mother figure, which manifested as subliminal grief. No one dared cry aloud for fear they would never stop. Although Daniel was only three when his mother "went to heaven," as he learned to say, her absence had a searing impact on him, leaving him adrift in an ocean of uncertainty and sorrow as he witnessed other children enjoying their lives with motherly nurturing. Mother's Day, birthdays, and even Christmas, with all its bright lights, triggered a kind of mourning period that the little boy could not explain.

As for Eric Bouchard, the family's patriarch, grieving was a natural course of life. He mourned his wife's loss so deeply that the mere mention of her name opened the floodgates of melancholy, causing him to throw every ounce of energy into his work, which he termed "my saving grace." When Michelle died, he vowed that he would never love or marry again—and he remained wedded to that idea.

As a pharmacist and owner of a pharmaceutical factory, Eric made a good living and kept his family in the upper-middle-class lifestyle to which they had been accustomed for many years. Material comforts and love, therefore, were the order of the day. Eric liberally showered each of his children with affection and attention.

For Daniel, his father was an idol—the perfect example of what a man should be. Every time Papa said "goodbye" as he left for a business trip, the four children would jump into his arms and overwhelm him with embraces. "Don't go! Don't go!" they cried, in unison, as the doting father gently pried their hands from his neck and rushed to catch his flight. Homecomings were just as sweet, with their maternal grandma, Amélia, frantically preparing her famous cooking for the occasion, including her delectable French butter cookies and madeleines.

Mischievous and playful, the little boys of the family could not wait to satiate their palettes with Grandma's scrumptious baking and would sneak up behind her to steal some of the batter. "If you touch anything again, Pierre and Daniel," she sternly warned them, "you are not getting a morsel of the baked cookies."

Sheepishly, the boys pulled their fingers away. Then, the instant Grandma turned her head again, they returned to their antics and gobbled more … and more, disregarding her admonitions. When hardly any cookies were left for Papa, he pretended not to notice, leaving most of the savory desserts for his children.

"Obviously, we have a mouse—or four, Mama!" he quipped, slyly winking at Amélia.

Despite enormous hardships, Eric Bouchard loved life, and to the extent possible, he did all he could to make his children feel comfortable and integrated into the world. This was not an easy feat without a coparent, but he did his best. As long as Papa was available and at home, bedtime stories provided a bonding experience, and the children would delight in curling up in his arms as he narrated. Their favorite story was *Le Petit Prince* (*The Little Prince*) by Antoine de Saint-Exupéry. The children especially loved the story of the rose and how the Little Prince viewed her as unique among all the flowers in the world. She was special because she was tamed—nurtured, loved, and showered with attention—just like the children.

Whenever his little ones were mischievous, Papa always had a remedy. Daniel, for example, never enjoyed school and would often make excuses not to go. "Papa, I feel sick," he would cry. Or, "Papa, my tummy hurts. I cannot possibly go to school today."

In tune with his children's habits and ever ready to employ his pharmaceutical skills, the benevolent patriarch would fill a vial with a vitamin concoction and say, "Okay, Son, if you are not well, I must give you this injection with strict orders not to go outside, play, or do much of anything."

Realizing that he would be cooped up the entire day at home, Daniel soon came to understand that pretending didn't do him any good at all. Besides, he absolutely hated the injection, and to avoid it, he ceased making up stories and always went to school—even when he actually felt sick. Thus, Papa effectively put an end to his shenanigans.

Then, suddenly, the enchanted world crumbled when the children found themselves all alone—just like the little prince—quite against their will. Daniel remembers one day in particular—a moment in time that changed his life forever. He was on his way home from school when a neighbor and fellow student approached and asked, "Is it true that your father died?"

"I don't know what you're talking about," Daniel replied, feeling his knees weaken.

The neighbor had known his family for quite some time, and Daniel knew that he was telling the truth. As it turned out, the neighbor's family told him the tragic news after seeing police cars outside Daniel's home. The walk back seemed to be a thousand miles or more, and it took the little boy all his strength to hold himself up, feeling as if he had been crushed by a wrecking ball. The world as he knew it had ended—forever. He felt like a nomad from another planet—just like the Little Prince, searching for meaning to a thousand unanswered questions.

Maybe he'll come back. There must be a way, twelve-year-old Daniel cried to himself.

"I want to come back to you, my son, but my body—my earthly form— is too heavy for me now." Eric's spirit resonated from inside his young son, as though it traveled through a million canyons.

As he trudged along, the tears fell like reservoirs. Grandma Amélia met her grandson at the door, sobbing. Then she gathered the four siblings in the living room. Holding each one close, she said, "You have had another great loss in your young lives. I am so sorry for all of you. I want you to know that I am here for you at all times. I am now Mama and Papa to you. Bury your sorrow in my shoulders and find comfort there."

For all of Grandma's kindness, however, Daniel, Pierre, Marie, and Collette were inconsolable. The siblings retreated to their rooms, each to individually nurse their gaping wounds. Whenever nightfall arrived, Daniel sat near the window, dreading the sunset. He recalled that his fictional contemporary, the Little Prince, tempered his sadness by watching sunsets, their orange glow giving way to seemingly endless darkness—until the next sunrise … and the next … For Daniel, however, nighttime was his nemesis, and he wondered just how many painful sunsets he would have to witness before his anguish would disappear and he would emerge from the pit of loneliness. He wished that somehow he could move to Norway where he could enjoy more daylight. In his moments of anguish, he failed to observe two luminescent stars, glowing together, smiling down upon him from above.

Chapter 2

Fitting into the World

When Daniel awoke after every sunset, he was enveloped with emotional anguish and felt as though he were a square peg in a round hole. He just didn't fit in. To make matters worse, his peers didn't accept him and bullied him constantly. Their taunts drove him to distraction and sent him into even deeper depression. They had parents, and he was orphaned—a status that made him feel apart from the rest.

One day, Daniel's bicycle broke down on his way home from school. Stopping in the middle of the road, with no one around, he let his tears fall freely. Suddenly, the sky heard his cries, and torrential rain poured down, as if heavenly angels were joining in his grief. Daniel was used to swallowing his tears and keeping his feelings in check. Yet, in that instant, he could not help himself. His uncharacteristic expression of distress was not caused by the malfunctioning old, rickety bicycle. Rather, it was a metaphor for the pervasive pain and loss in his life—the absence of his beloved father.

When he arrived home, Grandma Amélia noticed his distress and ran to embrace him. "Don't worry, my son. I will buy you another." She was always a lifesaver, and he did not know how he could ever manage without her. Though deeply moved by her compassion and love, the little boy knew that no one could mend what was truly broken—*his heart.*

As the years passed and he entered high school, things didn't become easier. Each year, on the anniversary of his father's death (March 5), Daniel would sit in his room and brood. The pain in his heart and soul was unbearable. *I don't fit in this life ... or perhaps, this life doesn't fit me,* he thought. *Is living only designed for pain and struggle? Does happiness really exist?*

As these thoughts pervaded the young boy's heart, he began to think about ending his life. He pondered the methods he would use and what he would say in a note left behind for his family.

Then, he restrained himself. The thought of his family was overwhelming. *How could I leave them? How could I break their hearts? That would serve absolutely no purpose.*

He thought of his brother Pierre, a mere teen who had been working day and night. For a time, he managed his father's pharmaceutical factory. Then, after selling it, he took odd jobs—anything he could find—just to support his siblings and grandmother. What would Pierre say and do if his younger brother committed such a rash act? He would be heartbroken. The tragedy of losing his father would be compounded numerous times over.

After entertaining these thoughts, Daniel decided, *No! I will not end my life. That would prevent me from fulfilling my mission. What that is, I'm not exactly sure yet. All I know is that doing right is manifested by a display of strength, and doing wrong involves showing weakness and self-doubt.*

This kind of thinking led him to plan his next step. He resolved to set out on an odyssey of self-exploration to prove himself to his family, the world, and himself. He would take his grief and rise from the ashes. *But how?* His high school grades were extremely poor, reflecting his indifference and disconnectedness from the world, which set him back a whole year, but he was ready to forge a new course and began to work hard. Slowly and steadily, through perseverance and focus, his grades began to improve. He graduated from high school with distinction, was accepted into a prestigious university in New York City, and prepared to leave home. His proactive stance inspired hope and aliveness in his heart again, and he had something to look forward to.

Naturally, the prospect of beginning a new life in a foreign land was more than daunting—especially for his grandmother, who gave him a whole list of dos and don'ts. His brother also sent him off with warnings of "Be careful and only associate with those whom you trust," and, "Don't get into trouble, and remember your roots. Think of what Papa would say."

"I always do," Daniel answered wistfully. "I'm doing this for him, for you, and for all the family."

In paternal fashion, Pierre took his little brother in his arms and embraced him. "Que Dieu soit avec vous," he said tearfully, while Marie and Collette clung steadfastly to their brother, never wanting to let go.

"Love does strange things," Daniel said. "It makes you laugh, cry, and find hope. I am going out into the world to seek my future and fortune. I'm striving to fit in, and I know that many promising things await me. I am doing this in tribute to all of you, and especially for Papa, who lived a noble life that was all too short. This is my chance to seize the moment and do what I can to create a better life for myself and make all of you proud. A change of atmosphere will be good for me, though I will miss all of you."

Blowing a kiss and turning away without looking back, Daniel felt a salty tear roll down his cheek. Then, summoning every ounce of emotional strength, he quickened his pace and ran to the bus station, from where he would leave on a flight to New York. Grandma Amélia quickly hurried inside, fearing that if she began to cry, she would never stop. As mentioned, that feeling was all too common in the Bouchard household.

Take me to my destiny and be with me, Papa! Daniel silently mouthed the words, feeling confident that somehow his father could hear and help him to manifest his dreams.

Chapter 3

Golden Days

The next few weeks and months were filled with excitement as Daniel acclimated to New York. The sights and sounds, though foreign to him, were strangely familiar. Everyone walked around in a great hurry and with intense focus, as if they were about to do something so urgent that the sky would fall if they didn't get there (wherever *there* was) in five minutes flat. Daniel found this behavior extremely amusing, and coming from a large city, he soon felt right at home. The true test of his resilience and ability to adapt, however, was the ease with which he mingled with people and found his place among different cultures and backgrounds.

As never before, Daniel felt a sense of freedom and self-determination and threw himself into his studies with enthusiasm and diligence. His specialty, engineering, was the perfect discipline for his mathematical mind. The students around him quickly engaged him in conversation, and although the languages and dialects were diverse, everyone seemed to understand and get along famously with one another.

At last, the orphaned boy from Paris had found his way in the world, freed from the isolation of his four-walled room. He now assumed decision-making control over his life and had a greater sense of self-worth. In no manner was he excessively proud, but rather, he was humbly confident, proactive, and energetic.

"Papa, I am doing this for you. Do you see me and what I'm doing? I want to make you proud," he would say aloud every evening before bedtime. Somehow, he felt that his father had a panoramic perspective of the entire world and was lovingly watching over him, guiding him every step of the way.

Occasionally, a group of students would take sightseeing tours to various cities and states and enjoy a much-needed reprieve from their studies. The Four Musketeers (as they affectionately came to call themselves) were seldom apart. Carmen from Peru played the guitar and set everyone to dancing, and Joshua from Washington State had a tenor voice that could mesmerize any crowd. Sue from China had a sweet, benevolent disposition that made her a joy to be around. She never met a stranger and was always at Daniel's side when he needed a confidante.

The purity of these connections uplifted Daniel's spirits and awakened him to the enormity of the universe and his place within it. No longer was he judged for who he was—a boy from a parentless family—but rather, he was known as a strong individual with a kind heart, doing his best to find his way in the world.

Daniel's excellent grades earned him widespread recognition among school faculty and students alike and gave him a solid foothold on his future. The respect that he received inspired him to learn and do more. He became a staunch perfectionist, always striving to "make it," as he always said. In fact, the only thing that he valued nearly as much as his true, enduring personal connections was his ability to get things right.

Amid this happy time of self-development and success, Daniel decided to return home to Paris for the Christmas break. He was brimming with excitement to see his family and prove to them that he had, in fact, made it, at least in the first half of his freshman year.

The family had been very skeptical about the boy's venture and his ability to survive on his own. After he left, Grandma Amélia lamented, "The world is cold. What will the boy do there, in that foreign city, on his own?"

"I am worried too, Mama," Pierre would say, "but we have to trust that he has a good head on his shoulders. I believe that he just wanted to show us that he could survive on his own. Relax and don't fret all the time. Daniel will be fine."

Finally, the day arrived when Daniel would come home. The whole family was in an uproar as if they were expecting a soldier to return from the battlefield.

"Silly girls, what are you doing?" Amélia teased as she witnessed the growing girls dressed in their finery.

"We haven't seen our brother in such a long time. We want him to see how grown up we are, and we want to honor him," Colette affirmed.

"I see. Well, that will not be difficult. You will always be Daniel's princesses, you know," Amélia replied tenderly.

After the girls dressed, Grandma Amélia, Pierre, and other family members from across town piled into two vehicles and drove to the airport for the reunion. As Daniel emerged from the terminal, shouts rang out from the little crowd of well-wishers.

"So, Mr. Man! You did it. You definitely proved me wrong," one cousin remarked. "You've made it out there, but I have to admit that you need a haircut."

Daniel laughed. "I know. You didn't think that I could live independently, but you need not have worried so much. I have met some wonderful people who treat me with respect and love. They are like family, and we look out for each other."

"Well, we are very proud of you, and we couldn't wait until you came home to us!" Marie wrapped her arms around her brother.

"Wait till you see all of the presents we have made for you," Collette chimed in.

"You look like Papa!" Marie exclaimed.

"Who are these beautiful young ladies? Have we met?" Daniel teased, admiring the girls' new dresses.

"How long are you staying, Son?" Amélia asked with joyful tears in her eyes.

"I will be here until New Year's Day," Daniel replied, hugging his grandmother tenderly. "And besides, I never leave you. You're as close as my heart." As he spoke these words, he looked deeply into his grandmother's eyes, observing her worn, tired appearance. Deep lines had appeared on her relatively youthful face, revealing the ravages of stress and grief. Yet, she was as lively as ever, promising him the best meal and dessert that she had ever made.

After these loving salutations, the family returned home and enjoyed a glorious Christmas holiday and New Year's Eve. They chatted and played games, opened gifts, and shared stories, songs, and laughter. Collette played the piano and sang in her most mellifluous voice, and Marie gave a small dance recital, allowing Fifi, the family dog, to join in.

Pierre and Daniel often sat together over the holidays and talked about everyday concerns and life in general. Of course, Papa entered into the conversation. "In everything I do, I think of him. The pain lingers and never disappears. It's part of me," Daniel observed sadly.

"Life is a difficult game, and you have to be strong," Pierre noted. "You know, you can come home at any time. The door is always open to you, and there are things that you can do here in Paris, the city of lights. You can study here too and enjoy time with your family. I know that you are happy, but no one can replace us." Pierre smiled and slapped his little brother on the shoulder.

"You are more than a brother to me. I look to you as a father figure. When Papa died, you stepped into his role and sacrificed so much. You put your studies on the back burner to support us. Don't ever think that I forget that fact," Daniel replied. "I know that this is my home, but there is no turning back. I'm doing well at school, and I cannot just leave my friends and my studies. My three best friends, Carmen, Sue, and Josh, mean so much to me. Carmen is from Peru, Sue is from China, and Josh is from Washington State. All have distinct talents and personalities that mesh so well with mine. They are creative, fun loving, and intelligent. At last, I have found my niche."

"I don't want to disrupt your plans and dreams," Pierre explained. "I simply want you to know that we are always here with open arms for you."

Daniel expressed reciprocal love and gratitude, promising to return at his first opportunity, perhaps over spring vacation. In those moments of comfort and joy, he never could have imagined what time would bring.

Chapter 4

Where the Memories Are

Having spent some time in the embrace of his family, Daniel returned to classes with renewed energy. The house in Paris held so much love and wisdom, along with a mixture of happy and difficult memories from his boyhood. In his mind's eye, when he took breaks from his studies, he envisioned himself as a boy sitting at the kitchen table with Grandma Amélia, who pretended to be illiterate so that her grandson could practice his lessons.

"I don't know how to spell that word. Show me!" the elder would say.

Daniel would dutifully comply, believing that Grandma didn't have a clue as to what his lessons were all about. Years later, it dawned on him that she was just employing a gentle, though sly, pedagogical method that would help him throughout his academic career: simplification through methodical explanation and repetition. Each time he didn't understand a concept or proof, he would say to himself, *How would I explain this to Grand-mère?*

Grandma Amélia was as much a lioness as she was a lamb. If anyone dared to look at one of her grandchildren in a negative light—or worse, attempt to harm them in any way—she would go on the attack with a fierce sense of righteousness. Her role as sole guardian gave her the right to assert her might, and no one wanted to be near her when her rare, but justifiable, temper surfaced. Being a staunch defender and protector of her family was simply who she was, even though her kindness and gentility were the most salient aspects of her character. As her grandchildren grew, she was as doting as ever. In her eyes, they would forever be children, and she would be eternally Grandma.

One day after class, just as Daniel was thinking of her nostalgically, he entered his dorm room and went to check his phone messages. One was from Pierre, who sounded breathless. "Please call me back as soon as you can," he said.

Immediately, Daniel picked up the phone and dialed home. His brother's voice was somber and trembling. "It's Grand-mère …"

"What has happened? Tell me quickly," Daniel said, lowering himself into a chair, feeling his heart race.

"There was an accident over two weeks ago … We didn't want to tell you, because we weren't sure about her condition, but …"

"Go on!" Daniel demanded. "How is she now?"

"She's gone, Daniel," Pierre blurted out, as if the sentence had been forced out of him.

"What? How? When?" Daniel froze. His breath was shallow, and he and Pierre just sat there on the phone and allowed themselves to weep together. Their entire lives flashed before their eyes.

"How did it happen? Daniel wanted to know, his tears streaming uncontrollably down his cheeks.

"There was an accident. Grand-mère and Cousin Mathis were on their way to a vacation spot in Marseille when, not far from home, a tractor-trailer turned a corner and hit their car head-on. Mathis suffered a concussion and a broken leg, but Grand-mère's injuries were far more serious. We held out every hope that she would recover, and the girls agreed that we should wait to give you news, because we wanted to tell you that she would be fine, but tragically, she didn't survive." Pierre broke out into sobs.

"I … I … cannot say … goodbye—not to Grand-mère. She was everything. I cannot remember living without her, and I cannot imagine my life without her in it," Daniel said joining in his brother's grief.

"I know, Brother. I know. She loved you very much. You must realize love never dies," Pierre said.

"I loved her so much … and I always will, until I draw my last breath. She will forever be in my heart. I wish that I could have come home, but that wouldn't have been possible because my passport was at the embassy, awaiting renewal."

"Please don't chastise yourself, Daniel. You had no idea about what had happened, and we made the decision to spare you the pain." Pierre tried to comfort his brother, adding, "I love you. Try to rest now. There is nothing any of us can do. You were her baby, and she adored you. Just remember that."

"I always will." Daniel hung up the phone in a complete daze. As much as he would have wanted to be at his grandmother's side, lack of timely knowledge and other circumstances prevented it. He was enraged at himself, even though he was not at fault. *I should have embraced her one more time when I saw her … just one more time. If only I had known that it would be the last time, I would never have let her go. She would remain in my arms forever,* Daniel told himself as he allowed the tears to flow.

The next day, Daniel told his professors and friends that he could not attend classes and preferred to be alone. He shied away from showing his vulnerability, wearing a mask of courage and never allowing the tears to fall openly. Naturally, everyone understood and expressed empathy in such trying times. For a while, he fell behind in his studies, and his grades suffered, but he tried to remain focused, despite the pervasive guilt that haunted him day and night. One salient characteristic that Daniel acknowledged about himself was that he could naturally forgive even the most significant wrongdoing *against* him, quickly forget all about it, and act as if nothing had happened. But when it came to forgiving *himself*, he was relentlessly intolerant. Thus, his guilt about not being able to go home to see his grandmother one last time gnawed at him like a parasite.

Fifteen days after he received the devastating call from Pierre, reality hit him like the greatest natural disaster—a tsunami combined with an earthquake off the Richter scale, coupled with a multitude of tornados—and that was just the beginning. For nearly a week, he ate only enough to keep his head above water, and if he slept a few hours, it was as if he had closed his eyes for a full night's sleep. His ability to communicate and interact with his friends diminished to the point that they felt tentative about approaching him. Deferent to his mourning period and deep depression, they respected his privacy. Still, they let him know that they were with him, especially Sue, who never failed in her attempts to make him smile.

As time passed, the gaping wound of grief began to become more tolerable, though it never entirely disappeared. Upon reflection, Daniel realized that Grandma Amélia would consider her life in vain if he became subsumed in mourning to the negation of his dreams—the dreams that her love and nurturing made possible. So he began to study more diligently, and his grades began to climb.

Still, in moments of solitude—especially during sunsets—the pain of loss was far too profound for his heart to endure. *How will I go on? What will I do? They say that lightning never strikes twice, but in my family's world, it has struck three times—with a vengeance. First Mama, then Papa, and now Grandma—all victims of tragic deaths. What is the meaning and purpose of life when good people die so cruelly and senselessly? Why is happiness so fleeting? Is suffering the only reality?*

As he pondered these questions, Daniel allowed one day to flow into the next, wearing a mask of courage and a painted smile. He began to engage with others again and even date. However, he never ventured beyond the platonic stage, and at the first sign of approaching commitment, he ran like the wind. His heart was still under lock and key, and he wasn't about to fall in love. *Love*—something for which he so yearned but had no definition in his world. Even the word itself was painful, synonymous with loss.

A year passed, and Daniel still had not returned home. His brother knew that this was due to his intense grief and the fact that the house contained too many memories. One day, however, Daniel finally mustered up the courage to board a plane to Paris.

Pierre, Marie, and Collette, all much more mature and worn with grief, showed up to meet him. The reunion was the antithesis of his last homecoming, with sorrowful tears flowing at every turn. The first thing Daniel wanted to do was go to the cemetery to visit Grandma's grave.

"I have to see her," he said. "I have to speak with her."

Naturally, his siblings agreed, and on their way to the cemetery, they stopped at a local florist to pick up some roses. Roses often have many connotations, and they can either be signs of joy or sorrow, reflections of positivity or negativity. When the siblings arrived at the cemetery, Daniel exited the car and headed toward the plot with a heavy heart. His siblings stayed back and gave him room to mourn on his own. The wound was fresher in his heart, and they wanted him to have alone time with Grand-mère. Kneeling down to place the roses on her grave, he spoke aloud.

"Grand-mère, it's Daniel. I love you. I am so sorry that I couldn't be at your side in your hour of need. You were always there for me and never let me down. I want you to know that you will be in my heart forever, and I will always strive to make you proud of me."

As he knelt beside the grave with one hand upon it, Daniel's tears fell like a torrential downpour. He touched his grandmother's headstone. He didn't feel the hard, immovable rock, but the soft touch of his grandma's hand. Slowly, he walked away, turning to blow a kiss. Then, wiping his eyes, he rejoined his siblings, and Pierre drove them home.

Upon reaching the house, Pierre held his brother by the shoulders. Daniel walked in, and in his mind's eye, he saw his grandma—a vision of goodness and strength. There she was, in the kitchen, baking cookies, pouring over his homework with him, smiling at the door as she waited for the girls to come home from school. There she was in the living room, tidying up the couch pillows and dusting the furniture. There she was, singing her favorite songs. He could almost hear her sweet voice, saying to the others, "Hush! Don't make noise! Your baby brother is sleeping." There she was, all around him, and he could hardly bear the sense of her presence, but he had to be strong. He had an obligation to fulfill.

Still writhing with guilt and anger at himself, Daniel sat on the couch and wept, clutching the pillows as if he were holding Grandma, while his siblings gathered around him. "She loved you so much. She wants you to go on with your life—to find happiness wherever you can. She wants that for all of us," Marie reassured him.

"Yes, what do you think Grand-mère would say if she saw you like this? She would say, 'Now, Daniel, my son, if you want me to rest in bliss and peace, you will do what I want and take care of yourself. You are grown now, and it's up to you to take charge of your life in the worst of times. I am not there to comfort you, but my love survives." Collette consoled him.

Daniel marveled at his sisters' compassion. After hours of collecting his thoughts and having something to eat, he resolved to sit down and have a serious conversation about the future with all three of his siblings.

"You may not know this, Pierre," Daniel began, "but the girls and I have been corresponding by mail, and we have broached the subject of selling the house."

"Oh, but ... I must stay here!" Pierre immediately protested. "I could not possibly leave. I have my work and ... My life is here. The girls are both engaged now to wonderful men. I have met them and entirely approve of their choices. They will be leaving here soon to begin their own families, and you are away at college. I, on the other hand, have nowhere to go. This is my home, where my roots are."

"Yes, I know. The girls have been filling me in." Daniel smiled for the first time, taking his sisters' hands. "I am so happy for them and so proud of the beautiful young ladies they have become. We have been thinking about selling the house—but only to you and no one else. We would never want you to be displaced. You have been our father and our rock all these years, and it's the least we can do to make this transaction with you ... at half price."

Pierre's eyes filled with tears. "That is just what Grand-mère would have wanted. This house will be preserved just the way our family has kept it for all these years. All of you can return at any time, and you will always have a home with me. Though our family is going separate ways geographically, we can still reconvene here, where the memories are. Wherever you are in the world, this will always be home."

The siblings embraced and wept, holding each other for a long time. In that moment of healing, Daniel knew that from that time on, his world would never be the same.

Chapter 5

A Solitary Rose

Daniel knew that his grief would not just vanish into thin air. He had to learn to incorporate it into his everyday life. After more reflecting and mourning, he began to mingle with his friends again, and they resumed their usual habits of enjoying free time and studying together. Often, they would go to the local coffee shop to talk and relax.

There, in the very same spot each time, Daniel saw a young lady with curly blonde hair and flashing blue eyes. Her only companion was a book. Daniel observed that she had an interest in Jane Austen's *Pride and Prejudice*. *That girl shouldn't be alone. She is so beautiful, with a lot to give of her heart and mind. Her eyes are so intelligent and luminous. She should be around people. Life is so much fuller and more meaningful in a group. I wish that she could join us. She is so solitary—like one rose in a garden of daisies. She truly stands out*, he thought.

There was something mystifying about the young lady—something inexplicable that captured Daniel's full attention. When she spoke, she had an indiscernible accent that appealed to him and gave him a sense of familiarity. Although his English had improved over time, he still had a decided French accent, and the fact that the young lady also spoke a different language made him feel a kind of kinship with her. *I wonder who this girl is*, he thought to himself. He wanted so much to talk to her, but he just couldn't work up the courage.

Then, one day, the group sat together at a table with an extra chair. Ms. Curly Blonde, as Daniel had secretly named the mystery girl, suddenly approached and asked, "May I borrow this chair?"

"Of course, but on one condition," Daniel said, blushing slightly. "That you join us."

The girl smiled back, took the chair, and left without another word.

Daniel had seen Ms. Curly Blonde in one of the university campus buildings before, but running into her at the coffee shop somehow made their connection real. *Is there a connection?* Perhaps, for Daniel was always asking himself, *Who is she?*

Two weeks later, as he awaited the arrival of his friends at the coffee shop, he spotted her sitting at her table. An empty chair conspicuously stood there, almost as if it were beckoning him.

"May I borrow this chair?" he asked courteously.

"Yes," the girl replied softly.

Daniel simply sat down, right in front of her. The girl was shocked, looking as though she wanted to say, "Who is this guy, and what does he want?"

Daniel had no idea how he mustered the fortitude to be so direct—almost audacious—but with all that he had been through in his life, he had concluded that when an opportunity presents itself, one must seize the moment. In his brief time on Earth, he had already learned that time waits for no one, and life is far too short. He had looked over and spotted the empty chair. His friends had not arrived yet, and he had some free time. Voila! *This is the moment. There are no second chances*, he thought.

Then, he experienced a moment of regret. "I don't want to bother you," he said, looking at Ms. Curly Blonde with some remorse. "If you want me to leave, I will. I am just joking around."

The girl glanced back with a certain air. "I know very well that even if I tell you to leave, you will find a way to come and sit here at my table. It's okay. You can stay."

"Thanks. I'm Daniel. May I ask your name?"

"Greta."

Elated to have an actual form of address for the intriguing girl, Daniel did not waste any time in asking the next question. "Where are you from?"

"Germany," came the reply.

After a moment's silence, Daniel ventured, "I know what the situation is like there, so I won't ask you from which side you come, because each side believes that the other does not exist. So I will just assume that you are from the middle of the Berlin Wall—both sides."

Greta laughed. "That's a good solution," she answered, feeling somewhat more at ease.

In the next instant, Josh, Sue, and Carmen arrived, and Daniel introduced them. "Please let's expand your table, and you can join us," Daniel offered.

Greta agreed, and an hour's conversation ensued. The new friends took great pleasure in their quality time together. For Daniel, not only had a small table been expanded, but so had his heart—with just enough space for a solitary rose.

Chapter 6

The Wall

Ever since he met Greta, Daniel's happiness increased in ways that he could not begin to express or analyze. That unique sense of being near her—the incredible sensation of butterflies in his stomach and sparks in the air whenever she was around—filled his life with purpose. It was more than the fact that he was growing up, and what he felt was *far* more than a crush. This girl had found the window to his soul.

Each time Greta joined the group of friends, Daniel felt exhilarated, but he sensed her hesitation to venture far from New York. Once, when the friends traveled to Missouri, she mentioned that she couldn't leave due to family concerns. Each time he or any of member of the group questioned her, she was evasive.

"I just cannot go away," she said. "I have too many commitments, and besides, I can only travel within ten to twenty miles from here. If I go any farther, my family worries about me."

The wall that Greta built around herself created an even more significant sense of mystery about her, inspiring Daniel to discover more about who she was and inquire about her family. The process of getting to know her was extremely challenging, especially since he didn't know how to interpret her need for nondisclosure and isolationism. *Is she rejecting me?* he wondered.

He couldn't tell exactly. There seemed to be chemistry between them, but Greta's elusiveness clouded her admirer's sense of security in their relationship—at least at first.

Essentially, the group of four had become five, but Greta seemed more interested in arriving about half an hour early to the group's gatherings at the local coffee shop, just to speak with Daniel alone before the others joined them. Often, they would discuss politics, and Daniel learned that Greta was from the German Democratic Republic (East Germany). Apparently, her father worked for the German government, but neither Daniel nor his friends could ever discover the precise nature of his role.

All Greta's admirer knew was that he felt good around her. She felt the same, although they did not speak a word of their feelings to each other or their friends. They simply shared a tacit sense of admiration and completeness that neither of them could describe. Sometimes, words fail to connote what the heart truly feels, and emotions are better left unexpressed—at least at the beginning of a relationship.

When words were insufficient, music found expression. Daniel introduced Greta to the music of French pianist Richard Clayderman, while she exposed him to the mellifluous sounds of Romanian pan flutist Gheorghe Zamfir. They listened for hours together, allowing their hearts to commune in chords and moods. When their cassettes clicked off, their hearts still pulsated to the sounds of budding love.

Soon, Daniel concluded that for better or worse, getting to know Greta involved breaking away from the group. In truth, her presence fractured the bond of friendship that the five friends had shared, but that was not Daniel's intent. He just wanted to know her on a deeper level. Because she was so private, having clandestine meetings without their friends seemed to be the only method of accessing her true nature and learning more about her life. Among the group, therefore, he felt some unrest, particularly from Carmen who secretly harbored unexpressed feelings for him, selflessly nurturing her emotions in silence, knowing that his heart belonged to someone else.

"Why must we always wait to order coffee until she comes, and why are you always talking about heading out with her alone? You must have feelings for her," Carmen would say with a tinge of sadness in her voice (and more than a small measure of jealousy).

"I just want her to feel part of us," Daniel reassured her, without knowing that Carmen's feelings were anything but platonic. With Greta, he tried to restrain any signs of romantic involvement (especially in front of the group), but he soon came to recognize that she reciprocated his feelings.

Gradually observing that Daniel's attention continuously wandered elsewhere, Carmen distanced herself from the group. When Daniel questioned her, she replied dismissively, "I'm busy. I have to study and eventually return to Peru. I have a mission of my own to pursue, and I cannot waste time diverting my attention from my goals."

Eventually, Joshua and Sue dispersed as well, only conferring greetings as they passed by in the hallways. Daniel understood that in some sense, he had alienated them by focusing all of his attention on Greta, but he had become completely immersed in spending time with her and could not stop the escalation of his interest. Love seemed to come at the price of splitting the group, and while he never wanted that to occur, he felt that he had to make the sacrifice to attain his greatest desire: Greta's heart. Later, he would come to regret such emotional estrangement from those who had meant so much to him, but as he would also learn, hindsight never served anyone.

However, as he matured, Daniel began to believe in the yin-yang nature of life and the inevitability of often extreme opposites—joy and disappointment, pain and fulfillment. Sadly, as much as he dearly loved Carmen as a friend, he hurt her by eschewing her affections. His heart was fully invested in the girl with the divine smile, and there was no turning back or trying to redirect his emotions.

Alone time with his love interest was of the essence, and one day, Daniel asked Greta to go for a walk in Central Park without the group. Springtime had touched the scene with its verdant new foliage and sweet-smelling air. As they walked along munching on huge soft pretzels, Daniel again broached the subject of politics.

"What does it feel like to live in a Communist country?" he asked.

"My family and I are fine because of my father's position," Greta said with her characteristic evasiveness. "I truly love the Western way of life," she admitted, "but when I go back to East Germany, I must keep my impressions to myself. Unfortunately, the government does not share them."

Her father must be an ambassador or in some government position, Daniel thought to himself.

Greta looked at him and ventured, "Because of my father's role, I cannot travel far away. Sometimes, I feel as though I'm being watched and monitored, but of course, I cannot let anyone know about that."

Daniel listened and basked in the joy of Greta's company but felt slightly uneasy at the thought of being scrutinized. Discreetly, he walked closer to her.

"You know," she said, displaying the usual brilliant smile that Daniel always admired, "I cannot have a serious relationship. There will always be a wall between us."

Daniel didn't know what Greta meant. "Walls mean nothing to me now—whether I encounter them in Berlin, China, or Central Park. I am here with you. No political strife or tension can ever disrupt this moment," he said tenderly.

"We cannot ever be anything but friends," Greta insisted.

Daniel didn't hear her words. His heart entirely rejected them. For the first time in his life, he felt that he was open to unconditional love. No longer was his heart under lock and key. This was not mere infatuation, but pure, untainted love that required absolutely no qualification. He was in heaven on earth. In Greta's presence, he could say or be anything or anyone he wanted to be—freely, genuinely, and without hesitation. Still, something within made him fear loss. Virtually everyone he loved with abandon had departed—his father, grandmother, and now … *No! It will not happen again,* he told himself.

Pausing, he pulled out a book from his briefcase, *Buch der Lieder* by the German poet Heinrich Heine (1797–1856), which he had purchased at the campus bookstore. He inscribed it with the words, *"With all my love, Daniel."* Nestled in the pages of the poem "Allnächtlich im Traume" ("Nightly in Dreams"), he placed a rose.

"Look at that poem and recite it to me," he said. I want to hear you reading those poetic stanzas.

Allnächtlich im Traume seh ich dich,
Und sehe dich freundlich grüßen,
Und lautaufweinend stürz ich mich
Zu deinen süßen Füßen.
Du siehst mich an wehmütiglich,
Und schüttelst das blonde Köpfchen;

Aus deinen Augen schleichen sich
Die Perlentränentröpfchen.
Du sagst mir heimlich ein leises Wort,
Und gibst mir den Strauß von Zypressen.
Ich wache auf, und der Strauß ist fort,
Und das Wort hab ich vergessen.

Daniel looked longingly at his new love. "Now, read it to me in English, so that I can understand the words completely."

Nightly I see you in dreams—you speak,
With kindliness sincerest,
I throw myself, weeping aloud and weak
At your sweet feet, my dearest.
You look at me with wistful woe,
And shake your golden curls;
And stealing from your eyes there flow
The teardrops like to pearls.
You breathe in my ear a secret word,
A garland of cypress for token.
I wake; it is gone; the dream is blurred,
And forgotten the word that was spoken."

"But promise that you will not forget any words that we have spoken together, my Sweet Rose," Daniel said.

"I will treasure this flower—and the words—forever," Greta whispered.

Time and again after that first meeting alone, Daniel tried to reveal his affections more and become closer, but Greta made it clear that even their friendship was only temporary.

"I have told you, Daniel. We can be nothing more than friends—*good* friends. You must accept that. My life does not permit anything else, even if … we feel it." She spoke the last words in low tones. "Even our friendship is simply in the moment—just like everything else in my life. My every move is monitored. Whatever I do, I don't have choices like other people. Choices are luxuries that other people take for granted. I don't expect you to understand completely, but if you truly care for me, you will at least listen to what I am telling you."

Daniel turned to Greta and kissed her gently.

"Don't think of the future," she said sweetly. "Let's just have this moment of enjoyment. We have today—*right now*—and that has to be enough."

Her declaration filled Daniel's heart with fear as he conjured his lady-love going off to another place and time zone without ever seeing her again. Later, however, it became clear that she could remain in New York to finish her studies, even if her family had to return to East Germany. (The call to return applied to her, as well as her parents.) That provided at least some leeway for the relationship to evolve. Still, a pervasive feeling of unrest washed over Daniel. Unwillingly, he perpetually lived in a gray zone without knowing what would happen from one moment to the next. In those times of uncertainty, he felt that his back was up against a wall without a ladder or any other means of climbing over or circumventing it.

Once again, love overwhelmed his heart and, predictably, was accompanied by pain. *How can I convince her to stay with me forever? Is that even possible? Is love a mere dream—an elusive mist that passes over and cruelly deludes me into thinking that it's real?* Sadly, the answers seemed beyond human comprehension—let alone one heart filled with love and longing.

Chapter 7

The Cruel Ocean

The next three months of Daniel's life were the most fulfilling in his memory. Despite the uncertainty that pervaded his relationship with Greta, their bond grew to such an extent that they began to spend more and more time together. Every sunny day and moonlit night was enhanced by their shared love. Sheltered in each other's embrace, they simply allowed the world to spin on its axis, silently bearing witness to their commitment and passion to the negation of all other associations.

Daniel was more than aware of the fact that his complete bliss and inner fulfillment came at the high price of losing his three closest friends who could do nothing but go on with their own lives, leaving him at the mercy of his enamored heart. In truth, nothing else mattered to him, and everyone close to him acknowledged that fact and just allowed life to move forward.

Without question, Daniel was in paradise. He felt that he could be completely free around Greta without standing on ceremony or trying to be someone or something that he was not. They walked, laughed, and even cooked meals together. She was impressed by his proclivity to concoct the finest cuisine from various cultures—Italian, Chinese, Lebanese, and French, along with many other delicacies. The two also ate out and introduced one another to their favorite cuisine. Greta particularly liked to frequent a well-known German restaurant in the area where she and her love went at least once a week.

Every day was another chance to rejoice and discover a mutual hobby or simply be in one another's company. Greta came to call Daniel, "my perfect man," and his name for her, "the girl with the divine smile," filled her with joy.

Soon, the two decided to live together part time, with Greta spending at least one or two days a week in Daniel's apartment on campus. Their mutual contentment resulted in the best grades for both, and they spent many hours together in the study hall, basking in quietude and one another's company. Sometimes, they sat quietly, and unspoken words gave way to a natural comfort and ease, as if they had known each other forever.

From what Greta had been saying about her father's circumstances, Daniel felt confident that he would remain in New York for a while with her family, and even if he had to return to Germany at some point, his daughter could remain in the United States until she finished college. Greta had the same idea and ventured to make future plans for purchasing a house and settling down with the man of her dreams.

When she spoke in those terms, Daniel's future flashed before his eyes—the most glorious sight ... ten, twenty, thirty years down the road with the woman he dearly cherished. Nothing could have made him happier. At last, love was approaching him with open arms, and he didn't have to shy away or be fearful of sunsets any longer. On the contrary, the waning sun beckoned deeper expression of the love that enveloped his heart.

What would have made him happier still (if that were at all possible) would have been a meeting between his lady-love and his family in France. However, because Greta was prohibited from traveling, he was content to meet her father at his opulent upper west side apartment. Greta happily agreed to a meeting and called her father to inform him of their impending arrival. Just the thought of interacting with her parents caused scores of butterflies to swarm inside Daniel's stomach.

When the day came, he drove to the designated spot and walked hand in hand with Greta up to the front door, resolving to be dignified and cordial, letting Greta's father know how much his daughter meant to him. As he stepped inside, he shook the stately man's hand.

"Daniel, I would like you to meet my father, Johann," Greta said proudly.

"Hello, it's a pleasure to meet you." Daniel seemed slightly tentative. As he looked around him, he observed a stylish living room adorned with artwork that appeared to be the creation of fine art masters. The floor-to-ceiling windows allowed refracted light to create a rainbow on one side wall. The atmosphere was warm and inviting, but there was something reserved and cautious about the gentleman of the house. Therefore, Daniel decided to maintain composure and decorum.

"You have a lovely place," he said politely.

"Thank you." Johann bowed slightly.

His demeanor shows that he is a politician. He probably has many layers to his character. I must be cautious, Daniel told himself.

"I would have wished to meet your wife, but I understand that she had to return to Germany for a while," Daniel added.

"Yes, she will be sorry that she missed you," Johann stated. "Our daughter speaks very highly of you."

"Thank you." Daniel looked at Greta and relaxed slightly. "I think the world of her."

"Greta tells us that you are studying engineering. That is very impressive. Tell me, what does your father do for a living?"

Daniel cleared his throat, trying to refrain from thinking too much about his family life. "Sadly, my father is deceased. He passed away when I was twelve. He owned a pharmaceutical factory."

"Also impressive. I am sorry for your loss." For a moment, a glimmer of empathy surfaced, and Johann's cool exterior softened.

"Thank you, sir. It was a long time ago," Daniel replied, trying to remain casual and in control.

The conversation continued for another half hour until the couple announced that they had to leave to prepare for classes the next day. Before they departed, Johann took Greta aside.

"He's a fine boy, and I can tell that you have profound feelings for him."

"I love him, Father," Greta said decisively.

"I want you to be careful. Nothing is certain, and it's not good to form attachments. You know that I—"

"Father, please don't say another word," Greta interrupted. "If you love me, you will not spoil this moment—or any moment of my happiness." She spoke sternly.

Hugging her father, Greta took Daniel's hand and left. "Don't mind Father's lack of emotion," she began when they reached Daniel's car.

"He's a very nice man. I enjoyed meeting him. Anyone responsible for your presence in this world has my deepest respect." Daniel sealed his words with a kiss.

Weeks passed, and the couple continued discussing their future. Winter was approaching, but the days were unusually mild, and their walks in Central Park became more frequent. Everyone who met the two were enchanted by their rapport and the way they finished each other's sentences. The only people who were a bit reticent about them were Sue and Josh, who would intermittently pass them on campus and wave slightly, as if they were nothing more than acquaintances.

"Love and regard don't only work one way," Daniel observed. "In a sense, I abandoned them."

"People move on, and we can't force them to feel as we do. Our love is very rare. We needed time and space to be alone and get to know one another," Greta observed.

"They believe that we did so at their expense, and Carmen just left without saying a word to me … but …" Daniel paused.

"*What?*" Greta asked tenderly.

"I have you, and that is the world," Daniel said.

"I feel the same!" Greta whispered.

That evening, Daniel prepared a surprise meal—a sumptuous lasagna with homemade bread. The couple dined by candlelight and watched a movie before Greta returned to her campus apartment.

The next day, Daniel awoke and ran some errands before classes began. When the whole day passed without a call from Greta, he began to feel a surge of doubt and uncertainty welling in his chest, but he quickly dismissed the sensation. Then, at about eight o'clock that evening, the phone rang.

"Hi!" Greta began casually. "I cannot speak with you right now, but I'm calling to ask that you meet me at the airport tomorrow morning at seven o'clock. Go to terminal 7."

Nothing in Greta's demeanor sounded unusual. In fact, she often made brief calls. The habit was part of her mystique. Daniel suspected that her father must have been in the room with her, and his presence prevented her from speaking. After pausing a moment to reflect, he hung up the phone and felt a sense of relief. *Good news. Her father must be leaving for Germany tomorrow, and we must see him off. Perhaps, without her father here, Greta will have more freedom,* he thought, as he prepared for bed that evening, drifting off to sleep after a few minutes of reading.

The next morning, Daniel rose early and headed to Kennedy Airport where, per Greta's instructions, he walked toward terminal 7. There, he saw Johann and three other gentlemen (whom he didn't know) boarding the flight. Simultaneously, he looked up and spotted Greta, who looked at him with an expression of intense resolve, devoid of emotion. She carried several pieces of luggage and just managed to set them down to wave her hand slightly.

"Flight 210 boarding from New York to Berlin, last call." A voice resounded on the overhead speaker.

Daniel looked straight into his love's eyes with an upward motion of his hands and a shrug of his shoulders, as if to say, "What's going on?"

Turning her head to avoid a response, Greta proceeded to walk toward the security checkpoint. Daniel stood motionless, as if frozen in time. Everything and everyone around him moved in slow motion, as the earth itself seemed to split in two, creating a cavernous rift between two worlds, divided by the vast expanse of the cruel Atlantic Ocean.

Is she going away, never to return? Was our love just a dream? Was she so heartless as to lure me into her heart, only to subject me to the emotional torture of her inexplicable departure? As these thoughts flooded his brain, he felt as though the entire terminal would come crashing down around him and succumb to the grief of his shattered heart.

It's like death, he thought to himself. *This is the third time in my life when loving someone deeply, with all my heart, caused me immeasurable pain. This may be my fate—my lot in life. No one could feel more overwhelmed and wrenched than I do at this moment.*

Daniel sank to the floor and held his head in his hands, barely able to move. A woman passed by, but he hardly saw her. "Are you okay?" she asked.

He nodded.

"Are you waiting for a flight?" the woman persisted.

"No, it's already gone," Daniel muttered incoherently.

Crouched against a wall, he remained there on the floor, waiting for his heart to slow down, oblivious to the passage of time. Time ... what did that concept—or any notion, for that matter—signify without her?

He must have been kneeling for about half an hour when, slowly, Daniel collected himself and rose to his feet. His legs were stiff as he ambled along, as though he were directionless. Somehow, he managed to compose himself just long enough to drive home. Upon arrival, he tried to avoid communication with everyone, even passing acquaintances, for fear that they would have detected his horrible secret—the destruction of his soul. Worse, they may have inquired, "Where is Greta?" The two had become inseparable and were rarely seen without one another.

Then, all at once, Daniel found himself in a different reality, one that he could not even begin to comprehend. He was entirely alone, and that was the way he wanted to be. For him, sorrow was like a kind of worship—feelings so intensely private, not to be shared. Like a monk retreating into meditation, he locked himself away from the world, seeking a seemingly unattainable cure for his broken heart. For an entire week, he remained in his room, leaving only to attend classes and then quickly retreating into his private sanctuary.

When Pierre called, he noted an unusually somber tone in his brother's voice. "You are not yourself. Are you ill?" Pierre asked with great concern.

"No, no. Please don't worry about me, Brother. You have your own life to focus on," Daniel said dismissively.

The truth was that he didn't want to speak with anyone—least of all his brother/surrogate father, who knew him better than anyone. He didn't want to explore his emotions for, in truth, he was numb. All his wanted was to hold Greta in his arms again, but she was nowhere to be found. He couldn't call her or fly to her. Most likely, she had returned to East Germany for good. *But why?* That looming question haunted him like the plague. In desperation, therefore, he took to pouring his heart out on paper. *I'll send letters to her home address in Germany*, he thought. Anger, sadness, and unrelenting feelings of love overwhelmed him.

In the following weeks and months, tons of messages left Daniel's hands—all in vain. As a result, he was adrift, as if at sea, without a life raft. Since the tragic departures of his father and grandmother, he had attained a measure of closure, and he was somehow able to integrate his grief into his daily life. The lack of closure with Greta, however, resurrected feelings of vulnerability again—the loss that always accompanied the investment of his heart and soul. Now, he was left to pick up the pieces of his broken heart.

Sadness turned to frustration, then to anger, and then to resentment, and lack of explanations left the young man feeling more confused than ever. Not only had he lost Greta, but also three of his dearest, most steadfast friends—for naught. He dismissed them, as though they were dispensable. Why? He was in love, and that feeling seemed to be mutual. Greta's affections were not a product of his imagination. Surely, he was not delusional. In fact, he did not doubt that his love was reciprocated. Still, there he sat … alone in his room … in silence. As time passed, her lack of communication completely baffled him, and absolutely nothing in his life made sense as a result.

As days and months passed, Daniel continued to feel lost, finding solace only in the quiet solitude of his room, hiding his grief from the scrutiny and questioning of those who knew him. Without his three closest friends, Carmen, Josh, and Sue, he felt as if everyone had abandoned him— especially the one he loved most. As much as he wanted to, however, he couldn't turn back the hands of time. While Carmen pursued her studies abroad, Josh and Sue remained at the university and immersed themselves in planning for their future, feeling betrayed by what they perceived to be Daniel's rejection. Each time he approached them, they casually greeted him, knowing that Greta had left. However, they chose not to question him or even engage in prolonged conversation. Their friendship had waned, and for that, Daniel felt deep regret—and pervasive guilt.

The most troubling, agonizing fact was that Greta was gone—for good. Back home in France, his safe, familiar place, Daniel's brother and sisters never ceased to worry about his state of mind. He may have been able to avoid questioning from friends and acquaintances, but his family knew him far too well.

"Daniel, please don't shut me out," Pierre begged him. "Tell me what's wrong. You can't keep your secret from me forever."

Choking back tears, Daniel replied, "Don't worry, Brother. I will tell you … in time. Just now, however, it's too painful to talk about."

In his state of perpetual disillusionment, Daniel sat down, almost six months after Greta's departure, to compose his final letter to her—a catharsis of his soul:

To the Only One Who Fulfilled My Dreams:

Greta, it has been nearly six months since you left and I first wrote to you, but you have not even sent a brief reply to explain why you departed. How could you be so dismissive? I have been trying my best to heal the wounds of my soul, but until now, without closure, I cannot move on. My soul has cherished you from the first day we met, and your name has been etched in my heart forever. My letters implored you to provide some answers to the many questions I had—and will always entertain—regarding your mysterious disappearance, without so much as a word of explanation. I have been patiently awaiting your return to my arms that could embrace no one but you in this world and the eyes that have not ceased looking for you everywhere—in crowds, on the street, in class, and even when I look at the stars. I continue to search in vain. I can barely refrain from breaking down over your loss. I am grieving, as if for one who has died. Yet, I know that somewhere out there you exist. I have sent countless prayers skyward and have spoken to the tireless moon to carry my grief and longing to where you are. That light beneath which we once walked together has dimmed for me now that you are not by my side, and despite my pleas and prayers, the good Lord has not brought you back to me.

Yes, I am hopelessly wondering … Why? That is the ultimate unanswerable question, to which only you hold the resolution. If I have done anything wrong or I have hurt you in any way, I am deeply sorry. That was never my intent. I promised that I would keep you happy forever, and I meant every word. I always wondered what would happen if I left you, but to my astonishment and dismay, the opposite occurred.

How could you ever have said I love you and then leave without a word or any explanation? You must have forgotten our beautiful walks on sunny days and beneath the moonlit sky. I do not doubt that you chose to dismiss all of this, including the fact that I loved you more than I loved myself.

I left everything and everyone behind, including the dearest of friends, for your sake, but you threw our love away and just walked out of my life. Everyone who sees me notices the grief in my eyes. They say that you placed in my heart the love that is instilled in hundreds of hearts put together, yet no one can ever even attempt to measure my eternal love for you.

Someone described you and your act of leaving as egocentric. As much as I don't want to accuse you of selfishness, I believe that the time has come for me to say, without hesitation, that you were, in fact, solely thinking of yourself, without any regard for the one who loved you most. We were planning a life together, and in an instant, you changed the course of our destiny. Without ever considering my feelings or the emotional destruction you would cause, you left me behind to pick up the pieces of my heart.

I will keep you in my heart until my soul ascends to heaven, even if you have decided to move on. Yet, I fail to see how this could ever be possible, considering the depth of love that we shared. I thought that I was the man of your dreams—your perfect man, as you always said. But now I have cause to disbelieve those words, for if I fulfilled that role, why would you have abandoned me?

With this final letter, I will put to rest the countless questions that have continued to plague me by day and night. By all appearances, it's over, but as hard as I try, I don't think that I will be able to look anyone straight in the eyes and say that I'm over you. The heart cannot restrain its reservoir of feeling any more than the sun can cease to shine. It's an organic process—part of the natural progression of days and nights, with and without you.

I wish you the best in life, Greta, and may you find joy and comfort in the people that you meet, including a romantic relationship that will last. But I hope you know that no one can love you with the completeness and depth of my soul that will forever be devoted to you—more than any love that can be measured in all of time, either by the full expanse of the cruel ocean that separates us or the measure of space between earth and sky. You will always remain in my heart.

Ich liebe Dich (I love you) …

Forever, Daniel

With that, the lovelorn man made a duplicate of the letter for safekeeping, put down his pen, and, for the last time, headed to the campus mailbox to dispatch the letter (which he sealed with a hint of his cologne), hoping that his once solitary rose would finally find a place to bloom contentedly—even without him.

Chapter 8

Family Schemes

Going home to Paris seemed like a foregone conclusion, especially since Pierre continued to barrage his brother with questions, knowing that he was in deep emotional pain. For his part, Daniel resigned himself to the idea that he would never see Greta again, and while she never provided a reasonable explanation, his final letter appeared to be a symbolic representation of goodbye — even if she never read a word of it.

The world was still baffling to Daniel, and all he wanted to do was escape. So when winter break rolled around, he boarded a plane at Kennedy Airport for Paris. Soon, he found himself amid the bright lights of Avenue des Champs-Élysées, feeling a strange sense of renewed inner peace.

Yet, when his cab pulled up in front of his brother's house, a flood of memories came pouring back like a torrential storm, reminding him of days gone by. All the sights, sounds, scents, and sense impressions of home brought back visions of his father and grandmother, and he could hardly contain himself. All at once, he mustered up the courage to put on a brave veneer and marched up to the front door like a battle-worn soldier coming home from the front.

"Brother, what is wrong with you? You don't have to put on a mask in front of me!" Pierre greeted him with a mixture of jocularity and somberness. "I know that you have a lot to tell me, and believe me, you will not get away with anything—not in my house." Laughing, Pierre slapped his brother on the shoulder.

"I'm so glad to be home, Brother. I love the familiarity of this place. It's where all my memories and my heart lie," Daniel said wistfully.

"But of course! What else did you expect?" Pierre beckoned him to sit down and gave him a cup of coffee. "Lots of sugar — just like you enjoy. You see, I don't forget a thing."

"Where is Adelle?" Daniel asked, referring to Pierre's wife. He had spoken to her on the phone but had not yet met her in person. Just after Grandma Amélia passed away, Adelle and Pierre were married in a private ceremony by a justice of the peace, with only Marie and Collette in attendance. Although Daniel wanted to return home for the occasion, Pierre discouraged the disruption of his semester coursework and advised him to focus on his studies. Now, however, the time had finally come for the siblings-in-law to meet.

"She is upstairs with baby Jacques. She will be down in a moment," Pierre replied before calling out, "Adelle, viens en bas[1]!"

Not a minute later, Adelle descended the stairs with her baby son gently cradled in her arms. A soft-spoken woman, Adelle nonetheless had an independent spirit, much like Grandma Amélia. Her kind brown eyes revealed that she would never harm a soul, either in word or deed. Diminutive in appearance, she also possessed enormous physical strength and health. She carried a rosy-cheeked boy on her hip, and he seemed to be as content as could be. A faint smile crossed his face.

Daniel rose to greet her. "At last, I meet my third sister!" he said warmly. "And my adorable nephew! Does he look like me, or am I flattering myself?" Daniel laughed for the first time in what seemed like forever.

"We have often said the same," Adelle observed. "I have seen your photos as a boy, and Jacques is almost your double."

Daniel smiled. The adults sat down together and indulged in a long talk, while Jacques looked around contentedly. Daniel told Pierre and Adelle everything that had befallen him with Greta, and in the process, he shed more than a few tears. The couple could not have been more supportive and encouraged him to speak his mind, even if he had to relive the pain.

---

[1] Come downstairs!

"Tears are like cleansing waters," Adelle said.

"There is peace in letting go, Brother," Pierre advised.

"You have the wisdom of someone much older than your years," Daniel answered admiringly. "I don't believe that Papa could have counseled me better, but ..."

"I knew there would be a *but*," Pierre said, smiling.

"Yes, you know me better than anyone. But ... it is easier said than done. With all that we have been through, it isn't easy to lose—over and over again." Daniel looked at his brother with a solemn expression.

"For you, the glass is always half empty. Think of what you *have*—here and now. You have so much love and acceptance from your family and your little nephew here who cries when he sees you—tears of joy."

Jacques had just begun to whimper. Daniel looked at his nephew and caressed his face.

"You know," Daniel said, wiping away some tears. "I am so proud of you. Look at you! You have such a beautiful family, a job that you enjoy—"

"Now wait," Pierre interrupted. "I'm a customs clearance agent, and my job pays the bills. Life just dealt me a hand, and I went with it. My incredible family—now that's another story. They make me feel on top of the world!"

"You sacrificed so much, forfeiting college and the job of your dreams all for the sake of your siblings, Marie, Collette, and me. We owe you a perpetual debt of gratitude." He rose to embrace his brother.

"All that you owe me is your happiness, and you would do well not to waste one moment in loving someone who is no longer accessible to you. Who knows what happened. We can speculate until the end of our days, and we may still never know the true story. Your love for Greta was what it was. It had a time and a place. Now, for your own sake and those who love you, you must move forward and fulfill your own life." Pierre's voice sounded eerily like their father's.

"Speaking of moving forward, how can you expect to do that without first taking a vacation?" Adelle interjected.

"A vacation? I am on vacation—here, with you!" Daniel replied.

"That's not what I mean," Adelle said slyly.

"Mon chéri, tell Daniel what you have up your sleeve," Pierre advised.

"A plane ticket to the French countryside (outside the gorgeous city of Vienne) for a week!" Adelle exclaimed jubilantly, producing the ticket from her dress pocket and handing it to Daniel. "Vienne is a place that you do not want to miss."

"Now, my sister, why would you do such a thing?" Daniel teased lovingly.

"Because I knew—we both realized when we heard your voice on the phone—that you were in an abyss of despair. That has to cease—*now*. Such is my wish. Also …"

"Yet another plan, my love?" Pierre smiled.

"As I was saying, Georgette, her brother, and parents are also staying in Vienne that week," Adelle continued. "At least once a year they take a break from work on their farm to go there."

"Georgette? Isn't she your friend Jean-Paul's youngest sister?" Daniel asked, addressing his brother. "I haven't seen her since she was a baby."

"I know, and she asked for you recently. "You will be surprised when you see her. She is quite a beautiful, engaging young woman," Adelle affirmed.

Pierre whispered inaudibly in his wife's ear.

"I don't know what you two are scheming, but given the fact that you have gone through so much trouble to get the ticket, Adelle, I must go and try to relax," Daniel said with resignation.

"There is no trying. Just do it!" Pierre stated.

"It was no trouble at all. We want you to take care of yourself. You have been in a web of grief lately, and you must disentangle yourself from it," Adelle instructed.

"My sister is as wise as she is beautiful," Daniel observed. "By the way, how are the girls?"

"When you return from Vienne, they have a surprise for you. I will say no more," Pierre said mysteriously.

"I stayed away for too long, allowing you to scheme at my expense," Daniel teased, immensely grateful for his brother and sister-in-law's concern.

The very next day, Daniel packed his bags and flew to Vienne where he would stay at a bed-and-breakfast to clear his thoughts—as if that were possible.

Chapter 9

An Interlude in Vienne

Upon his arrival, Daniel was struck by the quaint beauty of Vienne, which combined modern French and ancient Roman traditions. As he walked along the wide streets, filled with pedestrians, his eyes could not help but feast on the auspicious Roman Temple d'Auguste et de Livie and the ruins of city's medieval castle, Château de La Bâtie, nestled in lightly snow-covered mountains. The cloudless blue sky loomed large in the background, offering the promise of serenity amid the surrounding pristine beauty.

The scene starkly contrasted with Daniel's restless mind and heart, still writhing over his recent heartbreak. He could not help but think that perhaps, while he was away, a letter from Greta might have arrived. During his stay in France, he resolved to check routinely with the campus registrar for mail. *I don't care what anyone thinks*, he told himself. *A word from Greta would mean everything to me.*

As he walked along the streets at dusk, a young lady suddenly stopped him. "It has been a long time," she said shyly.

Daniel looked at her with a puzzled expression. "Do I know you?" he inquired, looking admiringly at the familiar face and flashing blue eyes.

"You knew me as a child. You used to call me *the baby*," the young lady replied.

"Georgette, is that you?" Daniel exclaimed upon closer scrutiny of the young woman's features. "Adelle and Pierre told me that you would be here, but I never expected to see you so soon. How you have matured! How is your family?"

"Thank you, we are all well. This is our favorite vacation spot. Jean-Paul loves coming here at least once a year, during summer or winter. He says that he loves to go back in time and visit the ancient ruins. Did you know that Vienne used to be a vital center of the Roman Empire?"

"No, I didn't. I haven't seen or discovered much of anything yet. I'm just here at my brother and sister-in-law's insistence. I've actually come here for a reason ... due to a kind of ... loss," Daniel stammered. "Pierre and Adelle, his wife, are forcing me to reintegrate into society and socialization, but I'd much rather not," he continued, trying not to show his vulnerability.

"Then, why are you here? You could have stayed in your room in Paris," Georgette replied.

"I don't mean any disrespect, but I just can't ... I don't want to talk about it," Daniel insisted.

"Oh, I'm so sorry, Daniel. I understand," Georgette said. "Would you like me to show you around? Perhaps a little tour will take your mind off things. It's okay. There's no obligation, of course. Nature is so beautiful here. Vienne is known for its spectacular sunsets. Besides," she added coyly after a brief pause, "a beautiful lady, à votre service,[2] can make you forget everything—even your own name."

Daniel laughed. "I will take notice of the sunsets and the lady, of course." Then, all at once, his expression turned solemn, as he recalled how alone and desolate he had always felt at nightfall when sad feelings seemed to creep in and overtake him.

Observing his sadness, Georgette ventured, "If you need a friend and want to talk, let's go for a walk sometime. I will gladly listen. In fact, I want to know what happened. Our brothers have been friends for such a long time, and you have known me since I was this high." She leaned to the side and pointed a couple of feet above the ground.

"You know, I'd like that very much. Venting might just be what I need right now." Daniel attempted a smile.

As the two parted, they agreed to meet the next evening for a walk

---

[2] "at your service"

through the city. Daniel was amazed that he had reunited with the little girl who initially struck him as simply the baby. *Time touches everyone*, he thought, *and it has been kind to little Georgette.*

As he walked back to the bed-and-breakfast that would serve as his lodgings for a week, he paid little attention to the scenic beauty around him. Though he felt somewhat relieved to engage his mind, his heart was still—and always—with Greta. Everything reminded him of her, even the air that he breathed. The weather was fresh and crisp, and the wind caressed his cheeks as if to say, "Wake up and see the glory and majesty of the world around you. Not everything relates to your pain and loss. Not everyone grieves as you do. There is still life and love to be claimed!" But he wasn't listening. He merely wandered, seeking in crowds to catch a glimpse of his lost love's face. No matter where he was, he appeared to be on the lookout, as if he would find her, by chance, in the most unexpected places—even in Vienne.

The next evening, he went walking with Georgette along the River Rhône in the center of the city. In early twilight, the weather was perfect, with the sun just beginning to set. Vienne's quaint houses and the bright-blue sky encircled them like a soft blanket. Just then, everything felt right with the world.

An expert on the region, Georgette later took Daniel to see the various tourist sites, including the Chapel of Notre-Dame de Pipet, whose magnificent glow in the evening moonlight would have dazzled the most disinterested passersby. Daniel, however, was indifferent, dwelling in a maze of emotional confusion. Witnessing this, Georgette tried to distract him further.

"How are the girls, Marie and Collette? I remember them too. They are so pretty and smart."

"Thank you. Both are fine. Marie is in the pharmaceutical industry," Daniel began.

"Like your father," Georgette recollected.

"Exactly. You have a wonderful memory," Daniel noted. "And Collette is a civil engineer, just as I'm aspiring to be."

"You must be very proud!" Georgette exclaimed.

"Yes, I am," Daniel replied with a distant gaze.

"Now, tell me: what about your breakup?" The young lady knew that it was time to change the subject.

"I thought you'd never ask." Daniel laughed with a sigh.

"That's why we're here, isn't it? To talk," Georgette remarked.

Feeling as if the weight of the world would come tumbling down upon him (just like the day Greta left), Daniel proceeded to recount his story. Georgette proved to be an excellent listener, interrupting politely at intervals to ask pointed questions. Daniel was impressed by her attentiveness and was grateful to have a caring confidante. Even though she was five years younger than he, she seemed to possess wisdom beyond her age.

"You know," she said, looking at him intensely, "you are not at fault, and you are not a person to be rejected. You have so much to give. This breakup is *Greta's* loss. You have had your mourning period, and it is *she* who should now reflect on her mistake."

"I don't know about that," Daniel answered with a slight chuckle. "I must have done something to send her away. The whole issue is driving me to distraction."

The conversation went on and continued for Daniel and Georgette's entire stay in Vienne, except for when he briefly met with her brother Jean-Paul and family. Everyone was amiable and welcoming. They inquired about his family, offered to show him more of the city, and invited him to stay at their chalet, but nothing Georgette's family could say or do managed to divert his full attention away from the sole object of his desire.

Before he knew where the time had gone, the week ended, and Daniel had to return to Paris, where he would remain with his brother and family for yet another week before returning to New York. Great surprises awaited him back in the city of lights, but the star-crossed young man still could not be consoled.

Chapter 10

Orchestrating Joy

"Daniel, as you know, our sisters have been engaged for quite some time, and now, they have a surprise for you," Pierre announced when his brother returned to Paris.

"Not that I will be an uncle again before they take their vows, I hope," Daniel replied, attempting some levity.

"No, nothing like that." Pierre laughed. "The girls will be here soon, and they will make their announcement. I hope that you had a good trip to Vienne. I understand that you met with Georgette. Isn't she a great young lady?" Pierre said, trying to divert his brother's attention from his brooding mind.

"Of course," Daniel answered, still unable to control his rambling thoughts.

"Look, Daniel, my boy," Pierre said in his paternal voice. "You have to pull yourself together. There is a whole world out there awaiting you. You cannot wait for Greta anymore. You must move on with your life, or you might as well dig yourself a hole and become a marmotte.[3]"

This set Daniel to laughing so hard that tears began to fall. "I don't

---

[3] Groundhog

know what to do, Brother. She was—is—the love of my life! How could she do this to me, and why would she just leave without even giving me a clue as to the reason?"

"I have great compassion for you, and I am here for you, but my best advice is somewhat harsh. I say this with love, Daniel. Do not allow yourself to be victimized by circumstance. The answer will, most likely, never come, and you have to let go. Without doing so, you will always be a slave to sadness and disillusionment. We have had great losses in our lives, and I became a father at a very young age. That was my job and my mission, and I was proud to step into Papa's shoes, but never believe that I did so without crying myself to sleep and talking to him every night. Then, after I allowed myself to grieve, I dried the tears—not only for my sake, but for you, Marie, and Collette. That was my only choice—*life over solitude, strength over weakness.* Living in misery would have been a kind of death, and so I chose to pick myself up and move forward. That doesn't mean that I didn't grieve. I still do, and I will for the rest of my life, but I will not allow it to overwhelm and keep me from living life to the fullest. Unfortunately, life is imperfect for everyone, sometimes filled with more pain and sorrow than joy."

Wiping away tears, Daniel rose to embrace his brother. In that instant, there was a knock at the door, and Daniel went to open it and greet none other than his two sisters.

"What beautiful ladies! To what do I owe the pleasure of your company? May I help you?" Daniel teased as he gave each of them a hug.

Not having seen their brother in a long time, Marie and Collette were in a flurry to greet him and tell him their news. Pierre had already filled them in on their brother's broken heart, and while they were eager to console him, they launched straight into their surprise.

"We know just the thing that will cheer you," Collette began.

"We realize that you have been so sad and alone, and we have conspired to organize our marriages around you," Marie chimed in.

"What are you talking about?" Daniel asked in amazement.

"We have decided to wait," Marie said.

"To marry until you graduate and can return to Paris to stay for a while," Collette interrupted.

"Do you mean to tell me that you waited all this time to marry so that I could be at your weddings?" Daniel asked.

"Wedding—a joint wedding," Collette explained. "Marie and Claude, Antoine and I are going to get married on the same day, and Pierre is going to walk with both of us in the procession."

"That is so wonderful, but—" Daniel began.

"Why is there always a *however* with you?" Pierre joked.

"It's just that I have a whole nine months before graduation, and that's a long time to wait," Daniel replied.

"We have already waited a long time to save up for a splendid celebration. Nine more months won't make a difference," Marie noted. "We can save even more for our dresses."

Collette laughed. "That is so true. You see, everything will work out, and you will be the best man for both of us!"

"Mon Dieu![4] You are a bundle of surprises, aren't you?" Daniel remarked.

"And perhaps you will have a date for the wedding," Collette said.

"You must be joking … and it's a cruel joke. My heart is breaking," Daniel said solemnly.

"I'm sorry, my dear! We want you to be happy," Collette replied apologetically.

"I understand that you mean well, and I'm deeply moved that you would orchestrate your lives around your unfortunate brother," Daniel said.

"I don't want to hear *but*," Pierre interjected.

"I am gratefully going along with this plan, and I promise to return upon my graduation—the very next day," Daniel replied resolutely.

"It's all set then!" Marie declared.

The next morning, Daniel packed for his flight back to New York, making a brief call to Georgette to thank her and her family for so graciously receiving him at their vacation home in Vienne. "The tour was wonderful, too!" he said. "I'm truly sorry that I was so distracted. I was genuinely glad to see all of you, but my mind was elsewhere, as you know."

"I understand. Think nothing of it," Georgette replied politely. "You will return fairly soon, yes?"

"In nine months for my sisters' joint wedding," Daniel said.

"Yes, I heard about the conspiracy." Georgette giggled.

---

[4] My God!

"I think everyone was in on it but me. To think that they're waiting for my sake!" Daniel answered wistfully.

"They love you. Everyone knows that, and why wouldn't they?"

There was something in Georgette's voice that made Daniel realize he was special to her—emotions cultivated by a time-honored connection, a bond initially forged by their brothers.

"I have to go," he said, "but thank you and your family for everything. I'm sure that I'll see you when I get back."

"I'm sure you will. À tout à l'heure!⁵ Georgette hung up the phone.

"Until then," Daniel whispered to himself, wishing that all goodbyes were so simple and straightforward.

---

⁵ See you later!

Chapter 11

Escape from the Past

Perhaps the hardest thing that Daniel had to do up until that moment in his life was to enter his empty campus apartment. He could hardly bear it. In his thoughts, Greta was still there, in every corner. He could even smell her perfume in the kitchen. Twice, to his embarrassment, he called out her name. Then he checked himself.

"I'm a madman," he said to himself aloud. "A madman who is still—and always will be—hopelessly in love."

Briefly, he considered seeing a counselor but decided that speaking to an impartial stranger would only serve to objectify his feelings and render them insignificant. He seemed to be defined by sadness—not that he wanted to be, by any means. Without closure, he simply could not extricate himself from grief.

As it turned out, no letters from Greta had arrived, and he resolved not to check his mailbox for two weeks. The box overflowed with ads and other school-related information on events, deadlines, and graduation parties—all of which meant next to nothing in his eyes, given his state of mind.

Just as he did when he first arrived in the United States, Daniel thrust himself into his studies to divert his thoughts. He reminded himself that he had returned to New York with a single mission: to finish his studies in record time—and he succeeded. In six months, he completed coursework that other students took more than a year to accomplish, thus exceeding his credit requirements for graduation. He accomplished the goal with the highest grades in the university for that school year.

During that time, Daniel was in constant touch with his siblings, preparing to return to Paris (three months earlier than expected), take stock of his life, and strategize the next steps toward his professional future. He was also delighted at the prospect of Marie and Collette's joint wedding and serving as their best man. Most of all, he was filled with the thought of how very proud their father would be that his children were creating their destinies after having endured so much tragedy in their young lives.

Time passed quickly, and as a last tribute to his experiences at the university and his bittersweet memories, Daniel visited the coffee shop where the friends had once shared so many good times and where he lost his heart forever to the girl of his dreams. In over six months, he had not dared to enter that place for fear of reminiscing too much. Once again, he wanted to attempt closure and say goodbye to his memories in New York—recollections that he soon would relegate to the past.

A few days before he left for Paris, Daniel made arrangements with Josh and Sue to meet at the coffee shop, their old hangout. As the three sat together at one of their familiar four-chaired tables, Daniel reflexively grabbed a chair, as if he were expecting Greta to arrive. Two of the chairs were conspicuously empty—one where Carmen used to sit and the other space that formerly belonged to Greta. It seemed sadly ironic that these empty spaces were once occupied by unrequited loves: Carmen, whose affections he had rejected, and Greta, the love of his life who had abandoned him without a trace.

Although the three friends were civil to one another, things were not the same between them. Their former good humor had been tempered by long absences from each other, and all of them were a bit cautious and tentative in expressing their true feelings. Nonetheless, they parted amicably and wished each other well.

Later, Daniel phoned Carmen at her old number, which had been disconnected. Then, after some investigating, he managed to leave her a voice mail at a relative's home. "I hope with all my heart that you will have a good life and find the right man with whom to share it. You are an exceptional person," he said. Breathing an inaudible sigh, he hung up the phone, never to speak to her again.

As doors were literally and metaphorically closing for Daniel in New York, other opportunities were opening, due to his excellent grades. A New York-based construction company with a branch in Dubai offered him a prestigious position in their company and gave him a month to make a decision. He felt conflicted and didn't even want to consider his options before speaking with Pierre, his trusted mentor.

Was it by chance or a stroke of fate that the young man left New York out of terminal 7, gate 12 at Kennedy Airport—the very spot where Greta had departed? He didn't know. Suddenly, snippets of the past four years flashed in his mind, a mixture of pain, loss, joy, exuberance, and exaltation. All in an instant, feelings of emotional upheaval came rushing back, and all he wanted to do was run away and leave the memories behind. In the terminal, Daniel tossed his cassettes of Gheorghe Zamfir and Ottmar Liebert into the garbage, as he imagined Greta doing the same with her Richard Clayton tapes. The music of love had been silenced.

I will never return to New York as long as I live, Daniel told himself, little knowing what life had in store.

Chapter 12

Une Femme Amoureuse[6]

Boarding the plane was far more emotionally difficult than Daniel had imagined. A torrent of memories came rushing back like taunting ghosts that wanted nothing more than to obstruct his path. Swallowing hard, the young man nonetheless moved forward, trying to compartmentalize his thoughts and divert his attention by thinking of his job offer in Dubai. He was leaning toward accepting the offer, but he still had a month to decide. All he knew was that he did not wish to remain in Paris. Instead, he dreamed of being a citizen of the world. The prospect of the new job, in an entirely different environment and culture, seemed very intriguing.

The city itself had a fascinating history, beginning as a desert and becoming a bustling metropolis. Located on the southeast coast of the Persian Gulf, this capital of the Emirate of Dubai, once known for its oil reserve flow in the 1970s, became a hub of business and commerce. In modern times, the city boasts the most beautiful, behemoth buildings, including the Burj Khalifa, the tallest building in the world (half a mile high). Even in the 1980s, the ever-expanding city, with its impressive,

---

[6] "A Woman in Love."

innovative technology, seemed like the perfect venue for Daniel to launch his professional career.

As his plane flew high above the clouds over New York, Daniel conjured Greta looking up at the same sky (probably filled with stars where she stood). At ten o'clock in the morning, the sun radiated brightly overhead, and the stewardess forecast more sunny skies ahead. Indeed, this had to be a good sign, but Daniel was perpetually immersed in contemplation.

The flight arrived at 7:15 p.m. in the city of lights, where a faint golden glow pervaded the horizon. Daniel was eager to rush to his brother's house, which he still called home, for a relaxing evening.

As usual, Pierre greeted him at the doorway. The loving energy that always pervaded that place was undeniable, and Daniel took it all in with a mixture of grief and gratitude.

"I'm going to see Grand-mère tomorrow. Will you come with me?" he asked his brother.

"Of course, I always leave two roses at her grave," Pierre remarked. "Somehow, she is always here with us."

"I know. I feel her presence here myself, and she is always with you, the father of us all," Daniel said tenderly.

The next day, after Daniel had a good night's rest, the two brothers went to their grandmother's grave, while Adelle and baby Jacques stayed at home. The wedding would take place in three days, and the family was trying to maintain composure amid all of the excitement.

After the brothers placed two roses each on Grandma Amélia's grave, Daniel asked if he could have a moment alone, and Pierre graciously obliged. As Daniel stood over the grave, looking at the name plaque, the sun seemed to beam at him from an odd angle, almost blinding him. Moved to speak aloud, he began a kind of monologue.

"I know that you see me, Grand-mère, and believe me, I never forget you—not anything about you, not any word that you have uttered to me. For my entire life, up to this very moment, I have tried to make you proud. I want you to know that I made it. I have accomplished my goals of graduating from college and being offered a high-powered position as an engineering manager in Dubai. I will probably take the job, as it gives me a chance to witness and experience another culture.

"As you most likely know, I was in New York for a long while, and there,

I met the love of my life—a girl named Greta—but for reasons that I may never be able to explain, she left me without so much as a brief explanation. My heart is broken, Grand-mère, and I know that if you were here, you would give me the best advice. Pierre has tried, but I have been inconsolable. I only hope that I can open my heart and love again, but having lost so many people—including you and Papa, both the core of my heart—I always feel abandoned, at the mercy of life's cruel twists and turns. Please, Grand-mère, if it is at all possible for you to guide me from your vantage point, wherever you may be, make the road smooth for your youngest, who loves you more than words can express."

As he ended this recitation, Daniel noticed the sun hitting him at the same angle again, causing him to shield his eyes. "Thank you," he said as he walked toward where Pierre stood in the distance.

"Let's go home, Brother," he said, feeling somewhat cleansed and lighter.

"Did you have a good talk with Grand-mère?" Pierre asked, smiling.

"Yes," Daniel replied softly. "I always do."

For the next few days, the family was wholly immersed in wedding preparations. Marie and Collette had already arranged the reception venue, a prestigious chateau near the Arc de Triomphe de l'Étoile, one of the most famous monuments in Paris.

Not only the location, but the wedding venue and all of the details of the event were planned meticulously by both girls and their fiancés, including the flower arrangements, the cuisine, the music, and the guests' seating arrangements.

Before leaving home, Daniel made special preparations for himself, purchasing the finest tailor-made tuxedo. After he settled in for a day, he called Georgette and asked her to be his date for the wedding. He considered her just a platonic friend who managed to divert his attention from his overwhelming sense of loss—nothing more. His heart was still guarded, but he thought that she would be a pleasant companion for the occasion.

"Will you attend the wedding with me?" he inquired on the phone.

"I thought you would never ask," Georgette exclaimed, trying to temper her exuberance. All her life, she had admired Pierre's younger brother, but due to his age and apparent maturity when compared to her, she had always presented herself to him as a little child, and that is exactly how he viewed her. Gradually, however, his eyes were opening, and she was hoping to earn his favor and admiration.

In truth, an undeniable attraction existed between the two, but Daniel did not feel the deep love and connectedness that he had experienced with Greta, and he doubted that his feelings could ever be replicated with any other woman. His heart belonged to her alone. Still, the hope of her return was a pie-in-the-sky dream, and it would be unfair to impose expectations upon Georgette. After all, she was her own person, with a unique set of traits and characteristics. To him, she had always been the baby from a hard-working agrarian family in southern France, but in the space of a brief time, since touring with her in Vienne, he sensed her inner and outer beauty, intelligence, and wisdom beyond her years.

Daniel hardly acknowledged that these attributes rendered Georgette the most eligible bachelorette—perhaps in all of Europe—and he did not allow himself to take note of them until the day of the joint wedding. On that occasion, she came to the close-knit ceremony at a small church near the family home, with Daniel, Pierre, Adelle, Jean-Paul, and another close friend in attendance.

Daniel was so caught up in the ceremony, the priest's blessings, and the radiance of his two sisters, that he didn't notice Georgette's quiet approach. He was thinking of Papa, Grand-mère, and the mother he never knew. So much loss was now subsumed in that moment of great joy. The presence of those lost was, no doubt, felt by the older brother/paternal figure and his wife as well. Daniel looked over and saw him light a candle and murmur something as if he were speaking with them. Adelle stood at his side, and when he finished, the two embraced and wiped tears from their eyes.

Suddenly, Daniel turned to look behind him. There, in the most stunning couture champagne-colored dress, complete with a Swarovski crystal bodice and a skirt accented by white roses, stood Georgette—an angelic vision. Her sparkling blue eyes offset the dress's brilliance, and she exuded utter poise and grace. Daniel was so mesmerized that he could hardly refrain from looking at her for the rest of the ceremony.

When the formalities ended, he offered her his arm, and the party entered a huge limousine that transported them to the reception hall. The place was adorned with flowers and lit by special lamps that reflected a golden glow off the walls. Outside the floor-to-ceiling windows, the guests enjoyed a glorious view of the Arc de Triomphe de l'Étoile enshrouded in moonlit radiance.

The guests soon sat down for a sumptuous meal, first featuring hors d'oeuvres consisting of cheese and fruit plates, followed by grilled fillet and salads of every kind. As vegetarians, the girls took care to please their guests but remained deferent to their credo that all beings must live.

Daniel could not help but discreetly glance in Georgette's direction all evening. As the live band played the joint wedding song, "Une Femme Amoureuse," Daniel gallantly led Georgette to the dance floor, with all eyes upon the pair (including the brides and grooms). Georgette blushed at the realization that they occupied the spotlight.

In the middle of their dance, Pierre brushed up against Daniel's shoulder. "If she doesn't make you forget Greta, I don't know who will," he whispered.

The festivities lasted until past midnight, and the guests were reluctant to go home. "I wish that we could stay longer. The aura is so wonderful here," one of the ladies remarked.

"I became young again tonight seeing Marie and Collette in such bliss," an elder gentleman noted.

As the festivities waned, the crowd dispersed, and Daniel and Georgette left, immersed in conversation.

"Would you like to walk with me in Jardin des Tuileries tomorrow?" Georgette inquired. I heard that it was designed by the same architect who created the gardens at Versailles. Is that true?"

"Yes, I know it well, and it would be a pleasure," Daniel said cordially, still trying to maintain distance, but feeling quite overcome by Georgette's beauty. "The baby has become quite a beauty," he noted.

"But I cannot replace *her*," she added, almost sorrowfully, focusing for a moment on her competition, still very much in the forefront of her companion's thoughts.

Daniel lowered his head without replying. Apparently, Georgette read his heart. She was not only intelligent, but beautiful, compassionate, and intuitive. Evidently, she liked him more than mere friendship allowed, but his heart was still closed, categorically rejecting any romantic interest … but … *How can I resist?* a little voice called out to him from deep within.

The next afternoon, on their walk through one of the most beautiful parks in Paris, the two fell into a deep conversation about life. Predictably, the topic naturally turned to Greta, when suddenly, Georgette paused in the middle of a flower field (looking quite like a flower herself) and said, "Listen, Daniel. We don't know where she is and probably never will. Why do you persist in speaking about her when she is not here? I am before you right now, yet you do not see me. You still envision her. You never ask about *my* life. You have to get over her, lift your head, open your eyes to the world and your heart to the possibilities that life presents to you."

These words meant so much to Daniel, and he understood what Georgette was telling him, in no uncertain terms. She was interested in him, and he would be a fool not to heed the signs. That's what his mind told him, anyway. His heart, however, was still very tentative and unsure. He reached out for her hand. "I understand. I do see you quite clearly, and you are a sight for sore eyes. You are also very perceptive," he said. "The baby is not only beautiful. She is also wise."

Georgette smiled. "You must promise not to call me baby anymore. I am a woman in your eyes. Isn't that so?"

Daniel agreed, attempting to focus entirely on her for the rest of the afternoon. The two spent a wonderful day together, and if there had been a hint of tension between them before, all reservations quickly subsided.

When Daniel returned home, Pierre admonished him. "Brother, forgive me, but I must tell you again and again: if you don't respond to this beautiful girl, whose heart is like no other and whose integrity is unassailable, then I don't know what I will do with you. You are blind. Believe me. If I were not married, I would date her myself!"

"My eyes are opening, Brother. Life has been complicated for me up until now, and I am still going through a lot of emotional turmoil. Where Greta is concerned, I cannot simply turn my heart on and off like a faucet."

"I understand, but you cannot victimize yourself either. You are cutting yourself off from the world and the countless possibilities that it holds," Pierre said sternly.

"That is precisely what Georgette said," Daniel noted.

"You see? She is brilliant too!" Pierre smiled.

"I noticed, Brother. Don't worry," Daniel replied resolutely.

Even though he felt quite sure of his attraction to Georgette, he was reluctant to characterize his feelings as love. To him, love felt very different.

It had an undeniable spark. It was synonymous with … *Oh, I must forget my self-pity and listen to the wisdom around me,* Daniel told himself.

After an extended, much-needed stay with his family, reminiscing and rejoicing with his siblings, Daniel decided to take the position in Dubai. "I must see the world and be a full participant in it," he affirmed.

Pierre agreed. "As long as you always consider this home."

"Of course I do! It's where my heart and my memories are. I was thinking—"

"I know, you are always thinking, Brother. About what now?" Pierre quipped.

"I have a commitment to Georgette now. Our relationship has evolved into a kind of …"

"Love?" Pierre ventured.

"I prefer to say a significant physical and emotional attraction," Daniel said, smiling. "You know that I'm not ready to say or feel that word yet."

"I understand, but you must not be so stubborn," Pierre urged.

"Well, I'm moving in the right direction. I was thinking of asking Georgette to come with me to Dubai. I have definitively decided to accept the position as engineering project manager."

"I am so happy for you!" Pierre embraced his brother. "And yes, asking Georgette is a wonderful idea. Let me tell you, Brother, you could not make a better choice."

Daniel nodded, still reeling from his own life-changing decision. He knew that Georgette had grown attached to him, and he had allowed himself to feel … *something.* She could not have been more attentive or doting, and he admired her shining qualities—physical beauty, intellectual capacities, and a kind heart. His brother was right, as usual, that he would have been a fool to let her go. He knew, however, that Georgette was a country girl, very close to her family, and wedded to tradition. He, on the other hand, was a man of the world, a traveler, and unanchored to any one place. Therefore, the transition to such an opulent city as Dubai would be far more difficult for her. With these thoughts in mind, he nonetheless ventured to pose the question on one of their walks.

"The opportunity is great, you know," Daniel said. "I have been waiting for it a long time, and I've worked very hard to achieve it."

"I am very proud of you, and I feel that my place in the world is with you—wherever you go. It will be a privilege to travel with you and to know that I will be at your side, my soul mate." Georgette reached over and embraced her new love interest.

Daniel's heart and soul filled with excitement, mixed with his usual guilt at the fact that he did not entirely reciprocate Georgette's complete devotion. Still, he could not help but melt at the sincerity and steadfastness of her soul. For her part, Georgette could not have been more ebullient and emotionally invested. In those sunny, carefree moments, she scarcely could have envisioned the trajectory that her life would take.

Chapter 13

A Sea of Possibilities

For Daniel, moving to Dubai was an exercise in deleting memories and wiping the slate clean—an entirely new beginning waiting for him, just around the bend. Although he always felt deeply emotional when he had to leave his family, he was secure in the fact that they would always be there for him. However, deep within, he had a burning urgency to leave everything that he knew behind and start again—just as he did when he left for New York. This time, he decided to be open to life and love, feeling intensely fortunate to have known the meaning of *true* love. While he acknowledged that it would be difficult to recapture that precise feeling of ultimate fulfillment, he also recognized the importance of freeing his heart from its prison of sorrow.

At first, he wasn't entirely sure as to whether his attraction to Georgette was real love, convenience, or the intense need to replace the love of his life in some fashion. She gave him every sign and opportunity that she was there for him, as if to say, "Open your eyes and see *me*, not anyone else."

At the time of his sisters' wedding, Daniel noticed and heard Georgette's plea for recognition. "Many others care for you, not only Greta. Life is filled with possibilities. Don't close yourself off," she told him repeatedly.

The young man was entirely flattered by the attention and found every kind of excuse to call Georgette while he was in Dubai, asking what color combinations he should wear and how he should peel potatoes and talking about the weather. For him, this was a prelude to commitment. The idea of merely having a girlfriend didn't appeal to him, however. In his eyes, the term and role of girlfriend were only temporary, and he decided that whatever commitment he would make had to be a complete engagement of his heart and soul. Also, the intensity and duration of his prospective union with Georgette were all the more significant, given their family connections and the fact that she was a traditionalist when it came to forging relationship bonds. The time-honored connection of their families, the close ties that her own nuclear family shared, and the desire not to disappoint his own brother loomed over his head like a thundercloud, and he did not want to make a mistake.

Always a loner, Daniel preferred retreat to interaction, introspection to engagement with others. It was not so much that he was antisocial. On the contrary, he always loved to share his joys whenever he could, either with friends or family, but when darkness descended (either of his inner spirit or actual atmospheric twilight), he reverted to solitude.

Somehow, he always felt a kinship to the sea, which seemed to emulate his inner dualities—calmness, with an undercurrent of tumultuous emotions, ready to burst forth at any moment. Fully aware of his changing moods, he decided to commune with nature and be alone with his thoughts in his new universe: Dubai. He was very fortunate, in that his company paid for his car and living expenses (including health care), giving him free reign to enjoy his off hours communing with nature, free of the pressures of city life.

With these intentions in view, he rented a house on the beach where he could sit out on his balcony and sketch the scenery around him—the sometimes calm, sometimes raging sea with its mysterious beauty beneath and often wrathful thrashing of waves against the banks at high tide. Infusing his heart in his sketching pencil, he gazed at the deep-blue sky above. Then, as he looked around him, he observed passersby and boats from afar, going to and fro, careening along the water at dusk, displaying tiny flickering lights. *I wonder where they are going to and coming from,* Daniel thought as the boats passed. He also loved stargazing and keeping track of the constellations that reappeared in the heavens from one night to the next. He enjoyed peace and quiet when he could give his racing mind a rest.

Daniel also thrived at work. He loved engaging in his assigned project: building the infrastructure of a small city with a view to expanding the area and connecting it to a larger venue. The shops and market areas, so beautiful to behold, were almost right outside his apartment, and if he walked just two minutes across the street, he could reach the beach and go for a swim. How he yearned to share all of this beauty with someone! *Would that someone last? Was she Georgette?* At least in his mind, her presence at his side would serve as a test of their compatibility and sense of connection to one another. The truth was that he did not want to be alone, and Georgette was his first opportunity to fulfill that mission.

"Come and see this place—this city away from civilization, so pure and clean!" he urged her on the phone.

"I'll come and stay at a hotel—or, on second thought, with my friend in Abu Dhabi. I'll stay with you for two weeks and then return to the capital and fly out from there." Georgette always had a knack for meticulously planning in advance.

"That sounds perfect. When will you arrive?" Daniel inquired.

"I plan to arrive within the next month," Georgette informed him.

In preparation for her trip, Georgette told her family that she would be traveling for a while to see a friend and would return within two weeks. "Don't worry about me," she told her concerned parents. "I'll be fine."

"It's a cruel world out there, darling, and your heart is pure. Just recently, you ventured away from home and farm life. Be careful, and don't take any risks," her mother warned her.

"You have taught me well, Mama. Please do not fear anything when it comes to me. I have my wits about me," Georgette said confidently. "I will call and write home frequently. In all events, I will probably return home before my postcards reach you," she added, laughing.

Georgette's parents were intensely proud of their daughter. Now of age, she felt that the time had finally come to explore the world—and remain at the side of the man she loved. When she allowed herself to feel for him, she could not deny that her future was with him. Still, she did not communicate her feelings to her parents or brother, for fear of being judged and told that she could not veer off the path of good sense, away from the simplicity of agrarian life. Until now, these ideas had guided her every step. Now, however, she did not want to allow caution to obstruct her destiny.

Seizing the day, therefore, she boarded a plane for Abu Dhabi, about an hour and a half's drive from where Daniel lived. Before she left, she revealed her plans to her brother Jean-Paul and his best friend Pierre who, in turn, hastened to call his little brother in Dubai.

"Listen well, Brother. Georgette will arrive for a visit. Don't forego this opportunity, and don't make any missteps. I know how you are and where your mind is. Just see the beauty for what she is and express gratitude, show respect. Do you hear me?" Pierre spoke in his most authoritative but loving voice.

"Yes, Brother," Daniel replied. "I will pay heed to your words. I know that you are so wise and are advising me out of pure love and paternal feelings. Papa would say the same thing. My heart is open now—at least, as much as it can be."

"Take care, Brother, and don't do anything foolish to ruin this moment. Georgette is a precious gem. Watch every move you make," Pierre repeated.

"Of course," was all Daniel managed to utter as he hung up the phone, feeling slightly overwhelmed. His heart raced, and he merely wanted to decompress and go out on the beach to clear his mind. *It will be so beautiful to share all this beauty with her,* he thought. *She appreciates the sanctity of nature as I do. I know that everything will work out.* With these thoughts, he comforted himself, taking time to quiet his mind and savor the moments in his place of sheer peace and tranquility.

Soon, when Georgette's arrival was imminent, he prepared to set out to meet her. The day was fresh and crisp, and the sun radiated its bright golden rays overhead. Each time the light hit his face through the open window, he heard his grandmother's voice. *The future is yours. Reach out and take it.*

Daniel was not going to allow this opportunity to slip away. As he drove along, he hummed one of his favorite tunes, "Une Femme Amoureuse," his sisters' wedding song. Before he knew it, he stood in front of an ebullient Georgette, who was waiting for him outside her friends' home.

"I'm so glad to be here!" she exclaimed. "This is such a unique and beautiful place. I have only been in Abu Dhabi for three days, but I truly love it here. The one thing that I immediately noticed was the scalding-hot temperatures! It's freezing at this time in Europe, so this is quite a change for me."

"Wait until you see what awaits you on the beach!" Daniel said.

"*Méduses?*"[7] Georgette teased.

"Don't be silly. Far more wonders than that. You need not fear when you are with me," Daniel said graciously.

"I already know that," the young girl said with a sweet smile.

The ride back was so pleasant and natural that Daniel did not think of the past for one moment. The conversation flowed as if the two had known one another for years (which, in fact, had been the case, but their association was quite different now). Daniel simply had not seen Georgette in this light before. No doubt, his perceptions were far more mature and born of experience. He was growing very fond of the girl who laughed at his jokes and looked at him as though he were an Adonis from Mount Olympus. Her respect and adulation were quite engaging, and he could not help but notice how charming and easy on the eyes his companion was.

Together, they took walks along the beach, stargazed, went on sand safaris—a magical experience of driving through dunes in a four-by-four, watching spectacular performances and upbeat musical interludes, all under a glowing night sky. They dined at less-than-upscale restaurants, where the prices had no bearing on the quality of the cuisine—rich foods, including fresh seafood, that filled the stomach in small portions and provided a feeling of strength and vitality. Daniel himself later admitted, "I feel ten years younger!"

A brief side trip to Oman, a country at the southeastern tip of the Arabian Peninsula, bordered by the United Arab Emirates, exposed the couple to distinct, fascinating culture, cuisine, and ways of life. Most of all, the two were deeply impressed by the kindness and hospitality of the people and their devotion to their customs.

Georgette was always in a state of wonderment, given that she had not traveled as extensively as Daniel.

"I'm a long way from our farm, and although I miss my family and my precious dog, Bijou, so much, I can really get used to this," she affirmed.

In this state of harmony and stasis, a platonic friendship quickly transformed into romance. Daniel's heart was completely invested, and he began to act as *un homme amoureux.*[8] Over the course of two weeks,

---

[7] Jellyfish.

[8] A man in love.

the two became more and more comfortable with one another. They even behaved like a couple, going furniture and appliance shopping together and choosing patterns for their home decor. Georgette had a very keen eye for interior design and freely made helpful suggestions about how to improve the appearance of each room. Under her guidance, the home and its once lonely occupant prospered. Daniel felt that this was a real sign of commitment.

She involves herself in my world as though she has been here forever, and I, myself, have barely arrived here. We are going through a new chapter of life together, and her opinions, likes, and dislikes appeal to me. She makes me feel so comfortable. This must be love, and no doubt, this is a commitment, Daniel told himself.

Time and again, Georgette expressed her love of the country, its people, and, especially, the company of her new love. "I told you," she said decisively. "You have so much to offer. The only thing you had to do in your life was open yourself to the sea of possibilities before you."

Taking Georgette in his arms, Daniel replied, "Yes, I see that now, and I don't just want to open my eyes for two weeks, two months, or two years. I want this to be forever."

"What are you saying?" Georgette asked, looking at him tenderly.

"I'm asking you to marry me." Daniel spoke these words with intense conviction.

Georgette laughed. "Hey, you! Silly boy! What took you so long? I knew that we were meant to be since your sisters' wedding, but you didn't notice me or listen to what I had to say."

"I did notice you, of course, but I was blind in many ways. However, I've become wiser in my old age," Daniel replied. "The next step will be to ask your father for your hand in marriage. In a few months, in springtime, I will take my annual one-month vacation and travel to your home for that purpose."

"Papa already knows and respects you and your family tremendously. The conversation will probably be very brief." Georgette laughed.

As the two embraced, Daniel felt that his life was finally on track again—at last, with someone to share life's ups and downs, joys and sorrows. With an open heart, not even the sky was the limit, and hopeful possibilities flowed like the sea at his feet.

Chapter 14

Trailing the Past Behind

Daniel counted the days until spring vacation when he would purchase a two-way ticket from Dubai to Paris. He could not believe that within a month, he would return to the United Arab Emirates, the place he recently called home, with his new bride at his side. The terminals through which he would pass could no longer stir up painful memories. The future was bright before him, radiant with hope and promise.

Still, he contended with smoldering emotions of uncertainty and the looming obligations that lie ahead. He wanted to be 100 percent committed so that he would not hurt Georgette in any way. In every sense of the word, she was a flower, sheltered from the storms of life by a loving family, who was also profoundly tied to him. He knew that once he gave his heart, there was no turning back, and he did not want to cause his family any hardship—especially Pierre.

To outside observers, as well as to those who personally knew the families, this was a match made in heaven. And as Daniel wrangled with peripheral doubts (that he didn't even admit to himself), he realized that by every stretch of the imagination, Georgette was perfect for him. There were absolutely no red flags and everything to love; yet, he feared *himself* and the hidden feelings that might surface when he least expected his heart to revert to its former state of unrest. Greta: an enticing albatross around his neck that lured him into past reveries of *what could have been.*

With all of these conflicting thoughts and emotions, Daniel subliminally tried to forget the past and invite his new love into his heart and future life. For the moment at least, that idea superseded everything, and he pushed aside the visceral feeling that Georgette was, in all her splendor, a replacement.

"Be sure of yourself and don't ruin our relationship with the family," Pierre advised Daniel again when he finally arrived in Paris. "I'm giving you this advice out of love. Georgette's family are the finest people you can meet anywhere. I don't want anything to go wrong. You're no longer a boy now. Be levelheaded and think twice before you leap so that you will not have any cause for regret. It's easier to back out now, rather than later. Think. Use your head."

"As usual, you are right, Brother," Daniel admitted. "Who wouldn't love Georgette and feel privileged to marry her? I am a lucky man."

"Just watch your step. I am here if you need a shoulder to lean on," Pierre said tenderly.

Daniel promised and went to lie down in his old room, where he remained the whole night. He slept soundly, and when he awoke, he went to the cemetery and had his usual conversation with Grand-mère. As per his custom, he poured his heart out, knowing that from her vantage point, his grandmother was listening and guiding him, sanctifying his impending marriage. Before he left that spot, Daniel placed two roses on the grave, this time representing himself and his fiancée.

Then, for the first time since Papa's passing, Daniel went to his grave. "Papa, I have been absent for so long, but this is not a reflection of how deeply I feel about you or the endless degree to which I miss you. I think it was too painful for me to return here to your resting place, but now, as Pierre has reminded me, I am a man, and I cannot shy away from my past, of which you were such a vital part. I am all that I am because of you, Papa, and I can only hope to make you proud the rest of my days."

As he ended this monologue, Daniel spotted a white feather at his feet. As he had become used to the idea of signs, he accepted this one as a matter of course. He knelt down, picked it up, and determined that he would present it to Georgette when he saw her.

That chance came three days later when he traveled to southern France, where her family had their farm. Everyone greeted him warmly, especially Georgette, who practically flew into his arms. She took the feather and placed it under glass, surrounded by dried roses.

How can I ever doubt my love for her? She is one in a million, Daniel thought to himself.

After Georgette's father, Hugo, had tended to his responsibilities on the farm, he beckoned his future son-in-law to sit down for a talk. "You know," he began. "You don't have to explain your presence here. My wife, Adelaide, and I are aware of your intentions with our daughter, and we could not be happier. You have always been like a son to us, and we have been one family for as long as we can remember. Your marriage to Georgette just confirms what we have known for nearly a lifetime: you two were meant to be. When are you planning the big day?"

"You must be clairvoyant—or maybe not. In two and a half weeks." Daniel laughed. "It won't be a large event. The most important consideration for us is that our beloved families will attend. I appreciate your kindness to me over the years and in this present, significant time in my life. I am a fortunate man." He embraced Hugo, handing him several gifts for the family that he had purchased in Paris.

"Thank you. We are delighted. We have never seen Georgette more radiant," Hugo noted.

"I cannot take credit for that." Daniel smiled and hugged his future father-in-law again, feeling a decisive pit in his stomach (for reasons that he tucked away in the farthest corners of his mind). The weight of commitment was becoming all too real.

As with all momentous occasions, the day arrived much sooner than anyone expected. Fortunately, the couple did not have to prepare too extensively. They planned to be married in Paris at Daniel's family's church and then celebrate at an upscale Paris restaurant, where they rented out a room for the afternoon and evening, replete with a band and the most sumptuous cuisine.

The day was memorable, and Daniel's family was very supportive, especially his sisters and their husbands. Pierre, as loving as ever, nonetheless kept a watchful eye on the couple, like a gendarme on a crucial assignment. Practically everywhere the groom went, he felt his brother's scrutiny.

"What are you doing, Brother? What is in that head of yours?" Daniel asked, finally addressing his behavior.

"I should ask you the same thing." Pierre chuckled.

"Listen, you are thinking far too much, and you know me much too well. I must ask you, as a favor on my wedding day, not to get into my head. Is that too much for a newly married man to request?" Daniel asked, half seriously.

"Not at all," Pierre replied, putting his arm around his brother's shoulder. "I just have eyes to see the metaphoric ball and chain of your past trailing behind you. It's that obvious. Please just listen to me, and don't pass that baggage along to Georgette. She doesn't deserve it."

"Brother, I don't know what to do with you. I understand that you mean well, but there has to come a time when you begin to trust me." Daniel affirmed.

"I most certainly will—when you learn to govern your emotions, let go of the memories that *were*, and focus on what *is*."

Smiling wistfully, Daniel walked away. *I am as transparent to my brother as cellophane*, he mused.

All night long, the bride took note of her husband's intermittent thought distractions and deliberately twirled around the dance floor just to divert his glance in her direction. She looked so beautiful and radiant that Daniel could not help but keep her in his sights, especially when she danced with her father. As she engaged the guests, he thought about whisking her away to Dubai and beginning their new lives together. He was so anxious, in fact, that he obtained her consent to travel directly from the restaurant to the airport.

Naturally, the families followed, and the bride said a poignant farewell, "Until next time," to her parents and brother. "I am never far away, and whenever you need me, I will be on the next flight," she reassured them.

"I know that my darling girl is in good hands. I never will fear, as long as you are with Daniel," Hugo said tenderly.

"You can count on me," Daniel replied confidently. "We have now solidified not only the marriage between Georgette and me, but an official union of our families—as we have always been."

Adelaide, the bride's mother, nodded in agreement and then turned away, as she could not bear to witness the couple departing from the gate.

All eyes were upon the two, wondering why a bride would board a plane in her wedding dress. "Nothing about us is conventional," Georgette admitted, observing the stares in her direction. "We live life like an art, seizing every moment, in living color—including white."

Everyone laughed and wiped their tears, mixed with joy and sorrow. Georgette grabbed her brother's hand and whispered something inaudible in his ear.

"What did you say to Jean-Paul?" Daniel asked.

"I told him that my dream was coming true," Georgette replied, embracing her husband.

Then, the couple joined hands and boarded the plane that several minutes later took off into a clear blue sky, as the groom did his best not to release his thoughts on the tailwind.

Chapter 15

Deliverance

En route to Dubai, the festivities continued, as the couple was lavished with celebratory cheers and well-wishes. Courtesy of Daniel's company, their tickets were upgraded to first class, where they were regaled with a cake and extra perquisites to suit their every need. All of their requests were met with grand ceremony and respect. Everyone complimented the beautiful bride and commented on how happy the couple looked together, and several glasses of champagne were raised in their honor.

Georgette (who never met a stranger) made friends on the flight and engaged in such lengthy conversation that Daniel teasingly reminded her, "You are married to me now, not the world." And he was glad of it.

Upon landing, Daniel's company sent a limousine to transport the couple to a five-star hotel in the center of Dubai. Their honeymoon lasted three days in a suite of indescribable magnitude, with the most breathtaking view of the city.

"I feel as though I'm in heaven!" Georgette exclaimed.

"Yes, we are, and you are its queen!" Daniel replied.

Georgette extended her hand, and in her sweetest, most down-to-earth manner, said, "Show me the world."

At that moment, feelings of pervasive love and commitment swept over the groom, and he faced his new life with joyful anticipation. No longer was he shouldered with responsibilities, but all of the joys attending marriage. His brother had been right, and he had chosen wisely. He felt that if this was what love felt like—more enrapturing than the sweetest dream—he never wanted to awaken.

Stargazing was no longer a solitary pastime for Daniel, who consumed every moment in sheer delight, holding the hand of the woman he loved. That feeling continued when, after their all-too-short hiatus, they had to return to the real world, as Georgette said. Daniel's projects required full attention, but he also managed to make ample time for his new bride to take her dancing and to dinner. Being more of a domestic, Georgette missed the chance to cook at home, but she never objected to living graciously and being served at her evening meal.

Daniel wanted to fulfill his promise to show his angel the world and took her to Singapore, Thailand, back to Oman, China, and Delhi, India, among other exotic places, whenever they had an opportunity—even on weekends. They knew that when they began their family, travel time would be limited, so they savored the sights as much as possible before settling in to a quieter lifestyle.

The couple's marriage was characterized by contentment and ease in each other's company, though Daniel's impetus to go out every night increasingly seemed to mar Georgette's inclination to nest.

My quiet life lies in the past now, Daniel told himself. *Somehow, I have to make up for the missing links to my happiness—and now I can.*

As for Georgette, her *raison d'etre* was to do anything and everything that would make her husband happy. His joy was synonymous with her own, so she would willingly surrender a peaceful night at home, watching movies or listening to music, for the sake of satisfying Daniel's wish to go out on the town. She did so without a hint of resentment or expression of discontent. Georgette noted, however, that she was always following along, never initiating or having a real say in anything; but she didn't object and accepted her routine with a full heart. She genuinely loved her husband, and he could not help but adore his bride, who was all goodness, light, and devotion. He would often say, "When it came to choosing a partner, I hit the jackpot."

Over time, all of Georgette's dreams of being a domestic were subsumed in satisfying her husband's wants and needs, which veered her away from the ideal home life in which she had been raised. More than anything, she wanted to have children, to be a mother and nurturer (which was, among other things, a salient aspect of her character).

Daniel, on the other hand, didn't entertain the same thoughts about fatherhood. Although he was not averse to parenting, his primary goal in having a family—at least, at first—was to solidify the marital bond and prevent his wife from leaving him. Children would be a means of securing his heart, such that any inclination on his wife's part to drift would efficiently be curtailed. It was evident that Georgette would never consider leaving him. On the contrary, she gave her husband every indication of her loyalty and unwavering love, but the boy whose heart had been broken countless times continued to live inside the man who still had a great deal of emotional growing to do. The very idea of loss was unthinkable to him, even though he knew that his wife had nothing to prove.

About eight months after they married, Georgette began to feel fatigued and slightly nauseated and told Daniel that she had to visit the doctor. "I'm just not feeling well," she admitted. Finally, she made up her mind to visit her primary physician to determine what was wrong. After her appointment, she approached her husband and announced, "We're having a baby!" She blurted out the words without any fanfare, fully expecting a jubilant reaction.

Taking her in his arms, Daniel said jovially, "That's funny. I didn't feel any morning sickness."

Georgette smiled. "Is that all you have to say?"

"No wonder you have been experiencing such unusual cravings," Daniel noted. His eyes displayed an air of complacency. In his heart, he felt grateful for having benignly locked his wife in, and in his mind, the forthcoming child was his security mechanism. Georgette could not turn back now. The feelings in the expectant father's heart could not in any way be described as indifference, but instead, *relief.* In truth, he could hardly comprehend the significance of being a parent. All he cared about was shielding his heart from further pain and disappointment. Unwittingly and innocently, his unborn child was the glue that would hold the marriage together. Nothing could take his love away now, and stability was ensured—or so he thought. He did not stop to contemplate his own role in actually making the marriage work, but instead, focused on fixing the union in stone, with no way out for his wife.

As for Georgette, she could not be more excited about motherhood. Every day, she conjured up little surprises for her unborn child, determined that the baby would want for nothing. She sectioned off a portion of the house as a nursery, painted the walls singlehandedly, and decorated most artistically. One of her friends offered to design a mural for the main wall, emulating her life on her father's farm. Daniel looked on with a mixture of amusement and apathy but could not overlook his wife's glowing appearance and demeanor.

"I hope that the baby will have your eyes and your intellect," she said.

"I am banking on the fact that he or she will have your looks and your wisdom," he replied.

"A combination of it all would be ideal!" she affirmed.

The two did not want to know the gender of their child beforehand, as they both hoped to surprise their families. The months passed without incident, and every night, as the child grew inside her, the expectant mother would sing her favorite lullaby, "La Petite Poule Grise."[9]

Georgette loved the feeling of carrying life inside her, and she wanted Daniel to experience the same level of joy; but each time she would mention the baby to him, she noticed a veil casting over his eyes as if his thoughts were far away.

"Tell me the truth," she said one day, deciding to confront him. "Are you not excited about this child? Don't you want to be a father?"

"Of course," Daniel answered softly.

There was nothing more to say. Time would bring feelings out in the open and would also foster greater understanding and maturity in the man whose heart was still very guarded. Being a patient soul, Georgette bided her time and remained focused and optimistic.

Just a few weeks before her delivery, she announced, "I want to have the baby in France. I miss home, Mama, Papa, and Jean-Paul."

"But this is your home now. Don't worry. You will be fine here, and besides, you are in no condition to fly," Daniel warned. "You have to take care of your health."

"I have been doing so all along, mon cher," Georgette reassured him.

[9] "The Little Grey Hen."

"I want to be with my family, and to be honest, I really miss the farm and little Bijou, my dog. I have not seen her in ages, and I'm afraid that she has forgotten me. Aside from this, I believe that Mama has kept my room as I left it, and I want to feel the familiarity of home again so that I can project that same security and love onto our child."

Daniel shook his head. "First, we must check with the doctor."

"My mind is made up. We must go to France. I will manage well. Nothing is wrong, and I want to take this opportunity. Besides, you should go home to visit Pierre, Adelle, and family in Paris. You know how everyone waits and loves to see you," Georgette declared.

"You are right," Daniel conceded, "but I will not feel at ease until we check with the doctor."

As it turned out, the doctor strongly recommended that Georgette stay at home and rest before her delivery, stating that traveling would be a risk. Nonetheless, the zealous mother-to-be went against medical advice and flew out of Dubai one week before her due date. For the next few days, Daniel attended to pressing projects and quickly took a night flight out to stay with his brother and sister-in-law in Paris. He slept on the plane, and when he awakened, he had arrived.

As soon as he opened his eyes, Daniel remembered that he was carrying a package that his friend and coworker Albert had given him to take to his mother in Paris, and he was determined not to forget that obligation.

Georgette's parents decided to rent an apartment close to the hospital where they planned to spend time with their daughter and care for her prior to her delivery. They secured a temporary dwelling where Georgette would stay, while Daniel opted to give her privacy and go home to be with his brother and sister-in-law.

After arriving in Paris, Georgette's father met them at the airport, and took his daughter home to their temporary apartment. Daniel rented a car and drove to his brother's home, gladly anticipating his visit. As he approached his brother's house, the paternal figure awaited him on the old familiar doorstep.

"It's so good to be here again!" Daniel exclaimed.

"Not half as good as it is to see you, mon frère, Pierre answered kindly, his face more mature, but every bit as wholesome, with age.

Daniel spent a few days with his brother and family and marveled at how the children had grown. At every opportunity, he made them laugh and spent quality time with them. "Uncle Daniel, you have a great sense of humor," Jacques exclaimed, chasing him around the room and challenging him to a pillow fight.

"You two are being silly," little Abigail, Pierre's four-year-old daughter, declared, jumping into her father's lap. "Papa, tell them to stop!" the little girl cried. "They are making too much noise."

"You are just like your great-grandma," Pierre said with tears in his eyes. "But she never wanted the noise to stop. She always used to say, 'I want life in this house. Just don't break anything!'"

"Okay, you can make noise. Just don't break anything!" the little girl parroted.

Everyone laughed, and for a moment, Daniel paused to reflect on what fatherhood would be like, but the thought was fleeting. On that score, he felt distracted and lost.

"I have to deliver a package from my friend to his mother, and then I'm going to stop at the cemetery. I have no time to waste. Georgette is going to deliver at any time, and I have to be prepared."

"Deliver what?" Abigail wanted to know.

"A baby, silly!" Daniel ran over to embrace his niece and then hurriedly left.

I hope the man is behaving, Pierre mumbled to himself. *He has a gold mine in that girl, and he doesn't even know it. He is still the boy with the broken heart.*

"What are you saying, my dear?" Adelle asked, seemingly reading her husband's mind.

"Oh, it's nothing, nothing," Pierre said dismissively.

Upon leaving the house, Daniel drove to the cemetery, and slowing his racing mind, he walked up to Grand-mère's plot. Kneeling down, he engaged in his usual long conversation, asking that she watch over his family, particularly the new life that was about to enter the world. Once again, an unusual angle of light seemed to strike his face, as if the lady herself were there, saying, "Never doubt me. Just because you don't see me doesn't mean that I'm not there."

That evening, Daniel returned home and called Georgette. "Don't worry about me. I must check into the hospital tomorrow, first thing in the morning. Time at home has been wonderful, and now I feel that our child is beckoning me. I felt two contractions last night," she informed him.

"Oh my God! Are you all right?" Daniel sounded frantic.

"I have never felt better!" Georgette said definitively. "Just get a good night's rest, and I will see you tomorrow—and so will your child." As the expectant mother spoke the latter words, she struggled to maintain her composure. "I am like a little child myself, awaiting the arrival of the greatest gift of my life!" she exclaimed.

In his usual measured fashion, the expectant father replied, "I know that Jean-Paul and your parents will be with you. You will be fine. Wait for me, and I will be there as soon as I can."

The next morning, Daniel rose slightly late and headed straight to his friend Albert's mother's home to deliver the package. The elder greeted him warmly. "How is my son? And what's this? What is he giving me?"

"To tell you the truth, I have no idea," Daniel said. "But just now, I am hurrying to the hospital, where my wife is going to give birth to our first child at any moment now. I will be in touch again."

"Oh, congratulations! Of course, please go and be careful!" The kind lady waved cordially as he dashed away.

That entire transaction took a full twenty minutes longer than expected. Then, en route to his destination, Daniel encountered unusually heavy traffic. "The hospital is more than half an hour away. I should have awakened earlier," he mumbled to himself, looking at his watch. He wished that he could stop and make a call, but he was trapped in the maze of vehicles surrounding him.

When he finally arrived at the hospital, a doctor came out to shake his hand, looking somber. "Mr. Bouchard, you are a fortunate man."

"Tell me what happened, Doctor. Is my wife all right? I came as soon as I could. I was stuck in traffic after delivering a parcel—"

Before Daniel could say another word, the doctor interrupted him. "Congratulations! You have a daughter." Then, looking pensive, he continued, "Your wife is all right now, but she and the baby were at serious risk. She was calling for you."

Filled with guilt, Daniel could barely speak a word. The truth was that his mind had been distracted, and he didn't recognize the gravity and magnitude of childbirth. He knew that he should have been there earlier, however. Had he taken the event more seriously, he would have been able to comfort his wife, but he became caught up in the moment of delivering ... what? What could possibly be more important than the delivery of his child? *My angel must have been terrified without me*, he thought, realizing his error all too late.

"What happened?" the beleaguered husband and father managed to utter again after a few moments' reflection.

"Georgette experienced abnormally low blood pressure in childbirth," the doctor began, "and just as the baby emerged from the birth canal, she wasn't breathing. The nurse had to administer CPR to revive the child."

Daniel gasped.

"It was touch and go for a while, but both of your little ladies emerged from the ordeal in good health, thanks to the expertise of one of our best nurses on staff."

"Can I see my wife?" Daniel's voice quivered.

"Georgette is extremely fatigued, but I know that she will be very relieved to see you. Personally, Mr. Bouchard, I don't know what could have kept you. Your wife gave birth one hour early, but you should have been here. Her condition was very delicate. Her parents and brother said that they had no means of reaching you, and frankly, they thought that something dire had happened. I'm just happy to see that you are safe."

"I'm so sorry ..." Daniel stammered, not knowing what else to say.

"She is in room 407. Enter quietly. We want her to rest with minimal excitement, if possible," the doctor advised.

"Certainly." Daniel shook the doctor's hand and went upstairs to his wife's room, as instructed. Taking the elevator alone to the fourth floor seemed like a slow boat to eternity. His heart was filled with regret, shame, and indecisiveness. *What will I tell her? How will I explain that I chose to deliver a parcel rather than arrive on time for the most significant delivery—the most physically and emotionally harrowing time?* Daniel lightly punched the wall, as if to chastise himself.

Then, the elevator opened. He walked down the hallway and entered Georgette's room. She turned languidly to look at him and extended her hand. "Mon cher, where were you? I was calling for you, but you didn't come. I tried looking around to find you, but you were nowhere."

"My angel, I'm so very sorry. I had to deliver a parcel for Albert ..."

Daniel said, leaning over his wife's bed, kissing her and displaying a bouquet of flowers, which he placed at her bedside.

"A parcel?" Georgette repeated in disbelief. Then, she smilingly said, "While you were delivering the package, I was delivering our bundle of love and joy, thanks to this lovely lady here. She also delivered our baby girl and me from certain disaster."

Georgette pointed to the nurse approaching her bedside, while her husband asked, "What is your name?"

"Annabelle," the nurse replied sweetly.

"That is so beautiful.' Daniel declared. "You are a true angel. Without you, my child would not have survived." His voice lowered, and he stood there, sullen and contemplative.

"Oui! Je suis d'accord."[10] Georgette's face brightened. "Your girls would not be here if it were not for this sweet saint."

Daniel stood motionless for a moment, as if he were trying to find himself again. The thought of what had happened in his absence to Georgette and his daughter was too painful to imagine. Then, his thoughts turned solely to his wife. "I must let you rest, and I will return tomorrow," he said, stroking her hair.

"Mama, Papa, and Jean-Paul were so concerned. They thought something might have happened to you. Jean-Paul finally left and said that he would speak with you later. All that matters is that we are all safe and sound. Our baby … what shall we call her?"

"What about Arielle?" Daniel offered.

"That is perfect. I love that name. It means Lioness of God," Georgette offered.

"That she is—strong and powerful, yet gentle and beautiful," Daniel said, feeling the hint of a connection to the child.

"Arielle is sleeping now, but tomorrow, you should come back and hold your baby girl. She wants to meet you," Georgette said with a smile.

Daniel could not believe his good fortune in having chosen such a gracious, understanding wife. Her placid reception was partially due to the fact that she was still very weak and medicated. While she was in labor, she felt dazed and in pain, and consequently, she couldn't acknowledge the full impact of her husband's irresponsibility. As for Daniel, no amount of

---

[10] "Yes, I agree."

blame could have plagued him more than the raging storms of guilt and remorse in his heart.

The next day, with a gift for Nurse Annabelle (as he called her) in hand, Daniel returned to the hospital. Sleep had eluded him all night, as a flood of thoughts swarmed his mind.

"Darling, you look exhausted, as if you were the one who had just given birth," Georgette said, smiling.

"I wish that I could have taken that pain from you, my angel," Daniel replied.

Georgette closed her eyes, as the nurse engaged the new father in conversation.

"These are for you," he said, handing Annabelle a bouquet of daisies.

"Thank you. I was only living up to the responsibilities of my job, but let me tell you what you already know: you have two very special ladies here, one of whom you haven't met yet. Wait right here, and I will return."

Within just a few minutes, Annabelle entered the room holding the baby girl in a pink blanket. "Here she is—your little princess."

At that moment, Georgette opened her eyes. "You see, she looks like her mother."

"Thank God for that!" Daniel laughed softly. "I don't know how I am so fortunate." As he held little Arielle, a million and one thoughts flooded his mind. The child was precious. *Is she really mine?* he pondered, still sensing a bond, but feeling disengaged as a father. He didn't know how he was supposed to feel or into what category of love the new child would fit in his life. The truth was that Daniel was on mental and emotional overload, with his heart and mind pulling him in many different directions.

In those moments, genuinely connecting with his little girl seemed impossible. He felt as though he were floating through the ether like a light beam, uncertain of his direction or purpose, focused principally on himself and his own goals. Deep within, however, he knew that the new life had liberated him in more ways than one — but he would not learn that lesson for a while. Instead, Papa (as Georgette occasionally called him) began to think of his next project management venture in Dubai.

"Just remember the doctor's strict orders," Annabelle warned him. "Your wife cannot travel for a full two weeks. She needs bed rest and nourishment, along with bonding time with your daughter."

"We can stay here in Paris, and my parents can tend to me while we are here," Georgette suggested. "I do not want to go against the doctor's orders. It is important for me to recover my energy and remain strong for our beautiful girl. In the meantime, you can also spend more time with your family here. It's a perfect arrangement."

In the temporary apartment, Georgette's parents set up a special room for the new mother and angelic arrival. Jacques and Abigail were delighted with to go and visit their little cousin (whom they called their sister) and took every opportunity to hold her and sing to her. The new grandparents doted on their daughter and new granddaughter with the greatest care and affection, and both never wanted for anything.

Daniel also frequently went to the apartment and beheld the entire scene with tender amusement, but his mind was always distracted by what would happen next in his career. When he was driving back to his brother's house, he brooded over his next step, realizing that he had a very important mission to address regarding work. That was his paramount focus.

Upon arrival, he immediately headed to his former childhood bedroom, where he sat and made a phone call to Georgette. Being in that place always calmed him, but in that moment, he was on edge. "Listen, angel, you have to understand," he began one afternoon. "I must return to Dubai very soon. I have an important project to manage, and I am needed there. We can return together. You will be fine."

"No, no! I am not ready. You know the doctor's orders. I am prohibited from flying for two whole weeks. I have only been out of the hospital for a little over five days. You cannot ask this of me," Georgette insisted.

"But, darling, I will be with you. There is no need to fear, and you know how important this project is. I have been waiting for it to begin for months now. I cannot shirk my responsibility to the company."

"The *company?*" Georgette was indignant. "I am your *wife*, your priority—and so is Arielle. Your responsibility is to us, our safety, and our security. There are more important things in life than project management. Arielle is your greatest project now! I'll tell you what you should do: go back to Dubai without us, and we will follow in a week or so. Then I will have time to rest."

"No! That is out of the question. I don't want you to fly alone in the plane without me. You have to be safe," Daniel replied.

"You are not making sense. You are so brilliant in business, but when it comes to family ... ah, mon Dieu! You say that you want my safety, but you demand that I fly before the doctor clears me. How is my life at risk if I travel at the appropriate time rather than earlier, at which point I might be in jeopardy? Explain this reasoning to me."

Daniel had never heard his wife's voice reach high octaves before, and he realized that he and his wife were in the midst of their very first argument. Trying to be measured and calm, he answered, "You see, I will not have you traveling with the baby without me—without any help. I want to keep both of you safe, and I can't bear to think of the two of you on that plane alone."

"You are being irrational. I don't know what has gotten into you, but I will be fine. There will always be people around to help, and if need be, I can ask for a wheelchair upon boarding. At least I will have more time to rest, which is crucial to my good health. If you truly love me, you will not make an issue of this, and you'll go ahead without us. I will meet you in Dubai in two weeks, at the latest," Georgette said decisively.

"I am sorry, but I cannot and will not agree to this," Daniel spoke imperatively.

"Ah, now your word is law. If that's the way you want it, if it's all about you, I will go along because I truly love you. I cannot say the same for you, as you would rather risk my health and be my knight in shining armor—for *nothing*—rather than follow the doctor's sound advice." Georgette said on the verge of tears.

"I will pick you up in three days, and we will go home to Dubai," Daniel said.

Silence.

"Hello?" he said.

Georgette hung up the phone and went to pack, trying to swallow her tears, never revealing her distress to her parents, but they knew what was happening. They felt that she was unhappy but could not bring themselves to believe that their son-in-law was anything but attentive and caring.

As for Pierre and Adelle, it was all they could do not to interfere in their brother's plans. "When that boy makes up his mind, there is no turning back," Pierre said. "His mind is a freight train, heading in all directions. He means well, but he never analyzes anything. He is impetuous and headstrong. I have to let him be, but I still have to keep my eye on him."

"He is a man now, and you have to let him make his own mistakes," Adelle advised.

"Not if his erroneous decisions involve that girl. She is the pride of her family—their treasure. I will not allow my brother to hurt her."

As these conversations took place behind closed doors, the days passed quickly, and before she knew what was happening, Georgette bid a tearful goodbye to her parents and her husband's family with the promise of returning soon with Arielle.

"Just think, she will be a young lady when you see her again," she said, feigning cheerfulness.

Daniel reassured Adelaide and Hugo that their daughter was in the best of hands. "We just have to return for the good of all of us. My ladies need the stability of home without worrying about traveling alone," he said, trying to reinforce his position.

In deference to their son-in-law and for the sake of their daughter's marriage and peace of mind, Georgette's parents said nothing. They just smiled demurely and proceeded to drive them to the Charles de Gaulle airport, scarcely aware of just how much the young couple's life was about to change.

Chapter 16

Hushed Whispers

In her heart, Georgette knew that something was not right in her marriage. For all his goodness, intelligence, and kind heart, Daniel was behaving as if the world revolved around him. Still, as a diligent, independent thinker, Georgette maintained her focus on her family and the new life that she and her husband had so recently begun together. During the flight home, she was sullen, almost depressed, having left the entire family so quickly and against the advice of her physician. She barely spoke a word, as Daniel immersed himself in an old movie.

Once they reached Dubai, they were happy to be on home turf, prepared to settle in and bring Arielle to her delightful new room that had been lovingly decorated for her. Communication between the couple had slackened considerably, as Daniel went out every night with friends and coworkers. Eager to appease him, Georgette hired Sophie, a live-in babysitter from France on a work visa.

By all appearances, life was blissful, as Georgette accommodated Daniel's every wish, and he entertained a mutual desire to please her. Difficulties arose, however, from the fact that his definition of pleasure and happiness was going out with friends, while she preferred to stay at home and enjoy her tranquil surroundings. With their goals at odds, it was difficult to maintain their connection.

On one occasion, in an effort to avoid what he called his wife's unnecessary isolation, Daniel organized an extravagant luncheon at a local international hotel for his colleagues and insisted that she attend. The main courses featured German cuisine. Georgette was perplexed. "Why are you so fixated on German food, Daniel?" she questioned him, recalling that his old flame had introduced him to that type of fare.

"Why not? Don't you like delicacies? You are planning to attend, aren't you, ma chérie? Please don't refuse. You will have so much fun. Besides, you shouldn't be at home all the time. We have only one life, and we have to live it!" Daniel insisted.

In her usual compliant manner, Georgette agreed to attend the event. "But you must promise me that you will never say that I should not remain at home. Our daughter is here, and she needs her mother ... and father. She is my life now, and you are her Papa. She needs to know you and—"

"Oh, don't be dramatic. Arielle will know me very well. There is time for that. All she needs to do now is sleep, eat, and heed the calls of nature. Her needs are very basic, and they are all met by our dear Sophie, who is here with her at all times."

Georgette shook her head. Clearly, this was not the kind of behavior she expected from her husband. She wanted him to be engaged and interact with her, not plan parties and stay away for long periods of time. The fact that he invited her to the grand event was very strange, in her view. How could she go anywhere with a baby in the house who needed her mother? Yet, for her husband's sake, she agreed and dressed in her most glamorous attire, looking as radiant as she did on her wedding day.

"Ah, you look gorgeous, Greta!" Daniel exclaimed.

"What did you just call me?" Georgette replied, blushing.

"My darling, what else can I call you but by your name?" Daniel said, embracing her.

"You called me Greta," Georgette insisted.

"What? No! Why in the world would I do that?"

"You tell me. That's what you said: G-R-E-T-A. I heard the name with my own ears."

Daniel knew that he had made the most egregious slip of the tongue, but he continued to smile and embrace his wife, protesting that he had said no such thing and extolling her beauty. "How was I so lucky as to find you among all the women in the world?" he said, taking her in his arms.

Deep inside, Georgette was hurt, but she brushed off the negative feelings, intent on having an enjoyable evening … and so she did. The couple danced a lot, and Daniel mingled, sometimes leaving his wife on the sidelines to watch—and wonder.

He is just like an adolescent boy, full of life; yet, he doesn't seem to settle down and be the man I know, love, and married, she thought to herself.

She was right. Daniel wanted to live as a single man, while experiencing the joy and security of married life—all without the commitment and responsibility. The question was, why? The answer: fear of loss. This did not make any sense, because he had no reason to believe that Georgette's heart would ever change. In fact, she demonstrated the opposite. She was as steadfast as daylight's transition into night; yet, his insecurities persisted.

"I just want to enjoy life. My heart is like a child's … I'm like Peter Pan," he would say, laughing.

Georgette found this somewhat amusing, but her patience was reaching its limit. When Arielle turned six months old, she announced that she was pregnant again. Later toward the end of the pregnancy, an amniocentesis revealed that she would have another girl. At the same moment, Daniel was clamoring to disclose the news of his promotion.

"That's wonderful, and I have something to tell you, my angel," he said excitedly.

"It can wait. What can be more important than this?" Georgette clutched her waist. "We will name her Claudette," she exclaimed.

"Yes, that is a beautiful name," Daniel replied.

"As I was saying, you will never believe it—or perhaps you will," he said, smiling. "I have been promoted to branch manager of my company!"

"Oh, is that what you have to tell me? Congratulations, darling," Georgette answered dryly, looking at the clock. "Why are you so late?"

"I'm not late. I just went across the street to the beach to celebrate with some people from the office," Daniel replied with a tinge of annoyance in his voice.

"I asked why you stayed out for so long. I have been looking up baby names all day with Sophie. My husband wasn't even here to share in the joy of choosing a name for our second child," Georgette answered sternly.

"Look, it is your choice to remain at home all the time. You could have joined us," Daniel insisted.

"*Us* should only signify you and me, not your whole group of friends. I want your time and attention, but you prefer to confer it to others." Georgette had a pained expression on her face.

"What are you insinuating?" Daniel wanted to know.

"Only that you have other things and people on your mind, except me. I heard Gheorghe Zamfir and Ottmar Liebert music playing in our room last night with the door locked. Sometimes, I feel like a prisoner in my own home, able to enter only certain rooms without feeling excluded and unwanted."

Daniel approached his wife and embraced her. "This is not us. We don't argue like this. It's just not meant to be. I'll tell you what. Why don't you go home to France and be with your family just before Claudette arrives?"

"What? Now you're sending me to France? Why would I require help from my family when I have all that I need here? You don't make any sense. Think about it. You brought me back home to Dubai when my doctor told me that it would be highly risky for me to fly, and now, before I deliver our second child, you suggest that I travel to be with my family. What can they do for me? This is my home. I will remain and have the baby here."

The raised voices and arguing made Arielle cry, and Georgette ran upstairs to tend to her, while Daniel stood in the middle of the room, without budging. He simply wasn't worried about his daughter. *She will be fine*, he thought. *The women will take good care of her.*

Quickly, he dialed a number and began to speak in hushed whispers. "Yes, I will. I will be there. Me too," he said.

When his wife came downstairs, she stood for a moment, listening and then asked, "Who was that?"

"Oh, just someone from the office," Daniel answered sheepishly, immediately hanging up.

The months passed quickly—at least for Daniel, who continued to socialize with friends, leaving Georgette at home, feeling abandoned. She kept her feelings private, however, always displaying a cheerful, grateful demeanor on the surface, establishing her world with Arielle and bonding with Sophie, who had become a good friend. As she observed Daniel's increasing emotional aloofness, she began to feel even more isolated, listening to Yanni ballads in their room, closing the door, and drifting into peaceful contentment. She also began to eat healthy, organic foods and resumed preparing meals at home. Daniel was hardly ever home for dinner, so she seized the opportunity to concoct whatever she wished. Often, when she would ask her husband to shop for vegetables and other groceries, Daniel would agree, but somehow always forgot.

"How difficult is it to remember to buy spinach?" she teased him.

"You know me. If my head weren't attached to my shoulders, I'd forget where I placed it. Work consumes all of my thoughts," Daniel replied.

The truth was that his new managerial position took up most of his time, but soon, for the sake of creating a harmonious home life and nurturing their love for one another, the couple decided to settle in and make a concerted effort to refrain from even the slightest hint of discord. They actually began to enjoy their everyday routine, rejoiced in their daughter and the prospect of their new arrival. Daniel resolved to be as attentive as he could and tried to be home on time after work, bringing staples and other necessities as required.

One day, he received a call from his friend Albert who, a few minutes into the conversation, inquired, "You know, I've meant to ask you how my mama was when you saw her. And did she like the caviar?"

"She seems to be doing fine and ... What? *What* caviar?"

"You know! The caviar you delivered. Is your memory going on you, my friend?"

"You mean to tell me that you gave me *caviar* to deliver to your mama? Do you know that I missed the birth of my first child, and it's all because of caviar?"

"Oh my God! I'm so sorry. I thought you knew." Albert sounded ashamed. "I never thought that you would choose to make the delivery just before your wife gave birth."

"It's not your fault at all, dear friend. It was my failing. I wasn't aware of the time. I learned my lesson, and I won't make that mistake again."

When Daniel hung up, he began to laugh uncontrollably. *It's time for a change*, he thought. *Life is too short and far too precious to put emphasis on things that don't matter in the long run. I have to focus and understand my purpose: to be a devoted father and husband.* In that moment, he truly believed that he had a new mission, and he was determined to stick to it.

The days and months passed quickly, and before they could blink, the crucial day of Georgette's second delivery arrived. This time, Daniel did not disappoint. He was at his wife's side, tending to her every wish—on time, 24/7, whenever she needed him.

He is beginning to change, she said to herself. *The man I so dearly love is returning to me.* She had never felt so happy in her life, and when Claudette was born, the couple bonded more than ever. Arielle was ecstatic to have a little sister and tried to speak and sing to her at every opportunity, even though she could barely form words.

In those moments of bliss, strife seemed a million miles away, but as the great poet, Kahlil Gibran (1883–1931) once said, "Your joy is your sorrow unmasked. And the selfsame well from which your laughter rises was often filled with your tears. And how else can it be?"

Chapter 17

Skin Deep

Fatherhood slowly grew on Daniel. Because he primarily related to business people—particularly engineers—it was initially difficult to make the transition into children's bedtime stories. However, his vivid memory of bonding time with his father made the process much easier, and he settled into a relaxed posture and inner contentment that he could not deny.

Georgette delighted in seeing the girls with Papa Ours,[11] as they lovingly called him. She often noted that fatherhood and domesticity became him and that he should consider wearing an apron, making dinner, and nesting even more often. For a long time, staying around home and being a domestic appealed to Daniel, but after a while, nervous energy began to set in, and he felt stuck in one place, as he always said.

Far sooner than he expected (and despite his attempts at steadfastness), restlessness set in again, and the new father became more interested in socialization than family life. He seized every opportunity to dance and drink the night away. In a sense, he wanted to relive his youth, always repeating how fleeting life was and saying, "We have to enjoy every moment before it's gone."

---

[11] Papa Bear

In moments of solitude, he thought of his past and how alone he felt without his father, but he justified his emotional absenteeism by telling himself that the girls were always surrounded by love. *I'll be able to know them, and they will become better acquainted with me when they are older. Besides, I cannot mentor them on matters about which only their mother knows—feminine subjects of which men are completely unaware,* he told himself.

These thoughts gave Daniel carte blanche to live with abandon and essentially insulate himself from commitment once more. At the same time, he was terrified of severance or cessation of devotion on Georgette's part. As she noted, "He is full of contradictions."

Before the new parents knew what was happening, Arielle turned two years old, and Georgette planned a birthday party for her in the backyard. Only close friends and family were invited, so as not to overwhelm the little birthday girl, who took every chance to sing to her guests, and all were eager to listen.

"In twenty years, she'll be at the Metropolitan Opera in New York City," one of the guests remarked. Everyone laughed, but Daniel seemed to be conspicuously absent from the festivities—at least emotionally.

Looking over at him, Georgette noticed that he was speaking with a woman she had never seen before. The lady had a pleasant smile and a gentle, positive energy. Daniel seemed completely engaged in conversation, speaking to her and stealthily glancing at her. Taken aback, Georgette nonetheless managed to maintain grace and poise, but when the guests filed out and she found a moment alone with her husband, she confronted him.

"Who is she?" she asked pointedly.

"Who?" Daniel asked with a slight smile.

"I'm not a fool. Who is she?" Georgette repeated.

"Oh, you mean Suzanne? She is my employee, a fine architect," Daniel explained.

"Is that all?"

"You might say that she is a friend."

"I might say a very close friend," Georgette insisted.

"Well, we only invited very close friends. What is this, the Inquisition?" Daniel turned red with annoyance.

"Your wife has a right to know, especially since you danced with her twice and only briefly with me. What am I to think?" Georgette continued.

"You can think whatever you wish ... and you will anyway, no matter what I say," Daniel replied cryptically.

"You are evading the issue," Georgette persisted.

"And *the issue* is?" Daniel sounded cagey.

"She looks like your German girlfriend, doesn't she? She has the same smile, a similar hairstyle, a decisive air of gentility. Can you deny it?"

"I must admit, you're right," Daniel said without more.

"So," Georgette began, moving closer, "does she mean something to you?"

Daniel slightly backed away. "Only insofar as she is a good employee and very pleasant."

"I see. Nothing more?"

"Nothing more." Daniel walked away, leaving Georgette's heart empty and wondering.

That evening, Georgette resolved to become a sleuth. Such conduct was entirely against her nature, but she just couldn't stop the incessant chatter in her head, telling her over and over again that her husband was unfaithful. Therefore, when Daniel called and said (predictably) that he would not be home for dinner, his wife set out to investigate. To her surprise, she found his wallet, lying in plain view on the bed. *This will be a good excuse to get him home,* she thought. *How did he not mention this to me?*

"Mon ami, you forgot your wallet at home. Did you not know that it was missing? You said nothing about it to me before."

"Yes, but I have been so busy all day. My friend kindly brought me lunch. After that, I had my head buried in spreadsheets and other documents all day long. I am exhausted. I will be home soon." Daniel hung up the phone quickly.

"I love ..." Georgette could barely finish her sentence. Looking around as if someone were peering over her shoulder, she slowly opened the wallet and, to her shock, found a contraceptive. *We never use this form of protection. My husband and that woman ...* She could hardly finish her thought without a flood of tears streaming down her checks.

Standing in the room alone, she sank to the floor.

"Mama!" came a little voice from the other room. It was Arielle. She had spoken her first word. Jolted by the timely interruption, Georgette lifted herself up and ran to her daughter's side.

"Ma brillante petite fille, vous avez parlé!"[12] she said. Wiping away her tears, she lifted Arielle in the air. All of her sorrows disappeared in an instant, but she was determined to question her husband when he came home.

At nine o'clock that night, Daniel walked in, feeling completely exhausted and unable to focus. It was not a good time to broach the subject, but Georgette felt that there was no other choice.

"What is this?" she queried, opening the wallet.

"It is ... what it is ..." Daniel replied, taking the contraception from her.

"Do you not have any plausible explanation? We do not use this type of protection," Georgette pressed.

"Yes, I know. It's just ... there ... What can I tell you?"

"The truth."

"The truth as it exists or as you see it?" Daniel questioned.

"*Stop!* Again, you are taking me for a fool."

"Not at all ... and don't raise your voice. Can't you see how exhausted I am?"

"Not as much as I am."

"Then go to sleep. Why are you looking through my things?"

"Your wallet was on the bed and—"

"What? Are you controlling my every move? Are you monitoring me? Are there surveillance cameras anywhere that I should know about?" Daniel raised his eyes to the ceiling.

Daniel had a way of making Georgette smile, even in a moment of heated arguing. She kissed him and walked away, swallowing her emotions and tears. That put an end to the contentious exchange—for a while. Then, a few weeks later, another incident occurred that gave her pause to question her husband's state of mind—and his loyalties. While she was tidying the bedroom one evening, she picked up a small piece of paper from the floor. Unfolding it, she read the words: "When are you coming into the office? I miss you, Suzanne."

"What is this?" Georgette asked when Daniel entered the room, handing him the paper.

"That's my secretary," he replied softly.

"The one who came to Arielle's party?"

---

[12] "My brilliant little girl, you spoke!"

"Yes, why?"

"It was hard not to notice," she snapped.

"What is it now, angel? Are you jealous again?"

"Do I need to be? I saw the way you looked at each other, the furtive glances, the smiles … It was all clear to me." Georgette lowered her head.

"I'm surprised that you are so clear. It's *nothing*." Daniel was becoming defensive.

"No? Then why is Suzanne sending you such overly familiar notes? I miss you? Does she have the license to say that to a married man with children?"

"I suppose that she can say anything she wants, especially when what she is saying is completely harmless. You are much too sensitive. You know I love you."

Georgette turned red with anger. "If you loved me, you would not seek or accept another woman's attention."

Without another word, she walked away, resolving to put the episode behind her, but over the next few weeks, her solitude became more profound. Daniel continued to arrive home at unusual hours without so much as a word. When her phone calls consistently went unanswered, she became suspicious. After much consideration, she mustered her courage and decided to show up unannounced at her husband's office with the excuse of taking him to lunch.

When she arrived at the opulent office building, Georgette marveled at the surroundings and the courtesy with which the staff treated her. This was her first visit to the place, although she had seen it from the outside on more than one occasion. Domestic life had kept her from visiting sooner, and aside from that, her husband's workplace seemed to be sacrosanct—a venue exclusively his own, away from family. Clearly, he was much admired by colleagues and staff alike, and an air of respect pervaded the atmosphere.

Georgette's heart swelled with pride as she was greeted like a kind of celebrity. "I will let Mr. Bouchard know that you have arrived. It is such a pleasure to meet you," the front desk concierge said. "All of us on staff saw your wedding photos from just over two years ago, and you are even more beautiful in person."

"Ah, you are too kind!" Georgette replied, feeling the burdens of her heart slightly lifting. Then, she quickly said. "Please! Don't inform him. This is a surprise."

When she went to Daniel's office, she was told to enter without accompaniment. "You are like family here, Ms. Bouchard, so you need not stand on ceremony," one of her husband's colleagues remarked.

Nodding in gratitude, she turned and glanced at Suzanne's desk and then noticed through a glass window that she was standing next to Daniel at his desk, very close to him. Drawing in a deep breath, she paused for a moment to observe the two. Their nonverbal communication spoke volumes. Suzanne tossed her head and laughed, while Daniel brushed her hair from her eyes.

Georgette had seen enough. She swallowed hard and resolved to be stoic—almost militaristic in her stride. "Good afternoon, darling!" she said, barging in as casually as if she had been there many times before. "It is a pleasure to see you again, Suzanne!"

"How are you, Georgette, and how are the girls?" Suzanne ventured, feeling a little self-conscious, yet trying to hide her embarrassment.

Daniel, who did not expect his wife's visit, stood there without saying a word.

"Nearly ready for high school," Georgette replied smiling, pulling out photographs of Arielle and Claudette. "Their dad is too often away from them of late. Projects abound, I suppose. Isn't that right, mon cher?" Her tone was almost ironic.

Managing to compose himself, Daniel walked over and embraced his wife. "Yes," was all that he could utter.

"I brought lunch," Georgette said, diffusing the tension. She was a charmer, and even Suzanne could not help but feel her graciousness. "Suzanne, please join us if you'd like. There is enough here—"

"Oh, no, but thank you!" Suzanne appeared flustered. "I have to go, but I'll see you tomorrow, Daniel. It was nice to see you again," she added, addressing Georgette, who rose to shake her hand.

Daniel knew what his wife was up to, and he was stunned. Never did he think that she would so boldly check in on him, but he realized that he had, in fact, been caught in the act—the act of being himself in her absence. For the first time, he felt ashamed. "We just had a meeting, and we were talking about a project. You know, since I became branch manager—"

"You must need to defend yourself. It is unprofessional for a boss to stand that close to an employee and bush the hair from her eyes. It appeared that you were sharing more than design plans for the building down the street," Georgette interrupted.

Daniel reached out for his wife's hand. "Thank you for coming here. I'm so glad that you did. You are the one I want to see—no one else. Please let's have a pleasant lunch."

Once again, assuming a posture of avoidance seemed so much easier than confronting the issues at hand. The two never wanted to argue, but more often than either cared to admit, they seemed to propel one another into a zone of discord. Georgette looked out the window in silence for a moment and then resumed the conversation, switching the topic to their daughters and the funny things that Arielle said to her little sister that morning.

For the moment and in the days that followed, Daniel seemed to be a bit more attentive, still coming home late, but just in time for bedtime stories. The girls were delighted and begged him to read their favorites, *My Rabbit's Tale* and *Friends Are Forever* by Dianne A. Rhodes and Mazen Kharboutli. In these magical fantasy worlds, it was easy for the loving father to immerse himself, forgetting his transgressions and having an idealized view of life through his daughters' eyes. Such happiness, however, simply masked their mother's pain, as she looked on, hoping that such family moments would always last.

Before long, more suspicious behavior surfaced, including low-toned communications. One evening, Papa Ours called to say he planned to come home early for dinner, but hours passed, and he didn't show. Georgette then decided to go to his office again—only this time, she remained in her car, undetected in the parking lot. There, not twenty feet away, she spotted him sitting close to Suzanne in deep conversation. For several minutes, the beleaguered spouse sat there in animated suspension, waiting ... As she continued to fix her gaze in one direction, she saw her husband lean in and give his companion a brief kiss.

Warm tears cascaded down Georgette's cheeks as she absorbed the scene. Quietly, she drove off. Upon reaching home, she got out of the car, wondering how she would handle this very difficult situation. Entering the kitchen, she took out a pad and pen and wrote the following note: "We saved your dinner. It's in the refrigerator. Just throw it in the microwave. Come and see me when you have finished."

It was just before midnight when Daniel arrived home. When he received the note, he had a sinking feeling in his stomach akin to what he had experienced when he lost his father. *I wonder what is on her mind. Is she leaving me? What can I do now?* he thought. Somehow, a different feeling of loss pervaded his soul—this time, the decline and possible demise of his marriage.

Slowly, he ascended the stairs and found Georgette sitting up reading a magazine. "Is everything all right?" he inquired.

"Perhaps for you, yes," she said softly. "I was there today. I saw you with her in her car in the parking lot. You kissed her. I witnessed it, and you cannot deny it." Georgette remained stoic.

"Yes, I did kiss her, but do you believe that gesture was anything more than platonic?" Daniel asked, trying not to panic.

"What is a wife supposed to think when she *knows* what she sees?"

"You don't know the circumstances. Loving someone as a life partner and comforting someone in need or showing compassion—"

"Once again, you take me for a fool, Daniel," she said, cutting him off. "I see the way you look at each other. There is a definite attraction between you, and you cannot get away with avoidance this time. As far as need, *I* am the one in need, and the *girls* need you. Your attention should be directed toward us. You seem to forget that you are no longer a bachelor. You want everything without assuming accountability for your actions. You will have the proverbial cake and eat it, irrespective of the consequences or realizing just whom you're hurting. I have nothing more to say." Georgette recoiled as Daniel reached for her. Silence prevailed for several minutes before she took her belongings and went into the guest room.

For the next two weeks, the silent treatment dominated the couple's marriage. Daniel found this to be insufferable and tried to cajole his wife with flowers, gifts, and cards of all types, expressing his undying love. Nothing that he did, however, seemed to move her—not even timely arrivals and phone calls during the day. She would simply not answer. At one point, she called him briefly to say, "Now you know how it feels," and immediately hung up. Finally, he decided to confront her directly before he left for work one morning.

"Ma chérie, I have gone out of my way to show my devotion to you. You know how much I adore you and the girls. There is no one else in my life. Please believe me. Give me a second chance," Daniel pleaded.

For the first time, Georgette spoke. "I will give you a second chance—on one condition. You must end your relationship with Suzanne."

"Believe me when I say that there was never anything between us, but just to prove my loyalty, I have sent Suzanne to an office in another city and hired a replacement. The young man is from the human resources department in my company and extremely competent. Everything will be strictly business."

Georgette smiled. "So you will not fall in love anymore?"

"Not a chance," Daniel interrupted, laughing. "Personal interaction should not be mixed with business."

"Maybe now you will understand that surface appearance is only skin deep. True and enduring love lies inside and sees through to one's soul," Georgette offered.

"Yes, my angel, and *I see you*," Daniel replied, taking his wife in his arms.

Once again, a union of hearts took place. Daniel vowed to place barriers on all of his work relationships and reserve ample time for his family. Nothing could have given him more inner security, except to fortify himself to face the unknown.

Chapter 18

The Search

In the days and weeks that followed, the family resumed their normal routine, with Daniel spending more time at work than at home. Still, Georgette felt more secure in his loyalties and steadfast pledge to family life. She believed in her husband's heart and intellect and felt certain that as he became more and more acclimated to family life, his ability to mature and settle down would be a certainty. Arielle and Claudette were growing beautifully, the mirror image of their mother, with her sensibilities and strong emotional makeup and their father's sense of humor and joy of life.

Although this feeling of normalcy comforted Daniel, he still wondered whether he had truly fallen in love or simply found a sense of security. One thing was certain: he didn't want to lose anyone again. In the back of his mind, he always harbored the fear that he would find himself alone, once again. His wife was an emotional Rock of Gibraltar and never gave him cause for doubt. Perhaps, on a subliminal level, Daniel simply did not trust *himself*.

Time and inclination for self-analysis, however, did not exist, and Daniel was not ready to face his own heart. Instead, he focused on becoming the kind of husband that Georgette deserved—devoted, attentive, and personally accountable.

As the couple bonded and delighted in their two girls, another joyful surprise descended on the whole family. Georgette became pregnant again, and soon, little Jean Pierre entered the world, named after his maternal and paternal uncles. The birth was uneventful, and once again, Daniel was with his wife, attentive and ready to accommodate her needs in every way possible. The girls were ecstatic to have a little brother to dote on and love. Arielle sang to him daily, and Claudette called him her little one, insisting that she was his second mama.

That year, the family vacationed in the United States for a while, visiting Disneyland in Southern California for two weeks. The excursion was planned in advance of Daniel's business trip to New York, where he was going to work on an important project for four days. Rides, comfortable accommodations, and views of the park delighted the family, and none of them wanted to return home to face their daily activities and Daniel's impending departure. Even a short journey away seemed like it would last forever.

When the family arrived home, Papa Ours returned to work and came home to his girls with a lovely surprise—two lovebirds in a beautiful cage. Arielle and Claudette squealed with delight, while their mother laughed and looked at her husband with a puzzled expression. "Where did you get these beauties? And why, if I may ask?" she inquired.

"I purchased them from a friend who was practically giving them away. I couldn't resist. They are so cute, and besides, they are symbolic of us," Daniel offered.

"Well, if you put it that way, mon cher, I cannot resist either." Georgette smiled lovingly.

"We shall call them Fifi and Bernard, and I will teach them how to sing!" Arielle declared.

"And I will show them how to play and be polite," Claudette chimed in.

The girls embraced their father and begged him not to leave.

"But I must. How will we feed the lovebirds if I don't go to work?" Daniel teased.

The next day, at the time of his departure, Georgette saw him off at the door.

"We will miss you, my love," she said. "It's better that you are leaving early before the girls wake up. They do not want to see you go. They will miss their bedtime stories."

"I will be home soon, and I will keep in touch. I promise." Daniel kissed his wife and departed swiftly.

That was the mother of all promises. He had, in fact, planned a four-day trip to New York, but he certainly did not anticipate where his mind and heart would lead him. After diligently devoting himself to his tasks and regularly calling home, Daniel suddenly disappeared. Phone calls went unanswered. Frantically, Georgette called the New York office, but Daniel had left, and no one knew his whereabouts.

It was beginning of 1990, and the world was in flux. The Berlin Wall had just collapsed three months before. Siblings, parents, their children, and others who had been separated between East and West Germany for almost three decades by the nearly twelve-foot slab of concrete suddenly and miraculously gained access to one another.

Now that the Cold War had effectively ended and the gate to freedom had opened, *Greta!* The name resonated in Daniel's heart. Gorbachev's *glasnost* and *perestroika* had taken hold, giving way to individual and collective liberation. It was an incredibly dangerous venture. All of Eastern Europe was under military surveillance and gendarmes populated the streets, wielding semiautomatic weapons. Who in their right mind would travel to such places during those times?

Knowing that his actions were foolhardy, Daniel nonetheless told himself, *Now is my only chance to find her and gain closure at last! I need … No! I deserve an explanation for her sudden departure,* he told himself.

Daniel knew that what he was about to do was impetuous, but he simply could not contain himself. He was not taking such an enormous chance for love, but rather for the ability to close a very painful chapter in his life. Even at the risk of his safety, he resolved to travel to Berlin and stay in an upscale international hotel, representing himself as a journalist so that he could blend in with the throngs of people and not incite suspicion.

As he did with many endeavors, Daniel decided to wing it. How he would manage to pull off the plan and conceal his French accent was, at first, beyond his comprehension. However, once he arrived in Berlin and checked into the hotel, he began to strategize. First, he went to the bar for a cocktail, and thinking quickly, he approached an affable gentleman with a journalist's badge.

"I know that this will seem like a very strange request, but I need your name badge," he said without mincing words. Daniel knew that he tended to be impulsive at times, but this was a risk that he would never have contemplated even in his wildest dreams.

"Why would you ask for that? I have never seen you in my life," the man responded in competent English, inflected with a German accent.

"That's a good question. You see, I have very urgent business here—a personal matter that has been lingering in my life for more than five years. I cannot explain fully, but believe me when I say that your help would be so appreciated. I promise to return the badge when I complete my mission," Daniel replied.

Naturally, the man had no reason to believe what he was hearing, and any rational person would most likely have denied the request. To anyone else, the specter of suspicion would loom everywhere, but in this instance, reason and human compassion collided. There was something is Daniel's demeanor—an earnestness and credibility—that the man could not deny.

"All right. I should be suspicious of you, but on the other hand, I have no reason to disbelieve you either. The odds are fifty-fifty." The man then proceeded to take off his badge and hand it to Daniel. "When you are finished with this, just slip it under my hotel room door. I'm in room 203. If anyone notices that I am not wearing my badge, I will just say that I misplaced it."

"I cannot thank you enough. You will have it back in no time. You can never know how grateful I am." With these words, Daniel finished his cocktail and retired to his room, going through the motions of personal hygiene and collapsing into bed. Millions of thoughts pervaded his mind, but he was much too tired to pay heed. He must have slept more than he thought, because when his alarm rang at ten thirty the next morning, he bounded out of bed as if he were late for an appointment. He had no time to waste, as he had to take a flight out to Dubai the next evening.

Oh, what Georgette must be thinking! How am I going to explain myself? Daniel mumbled nervously to himself.

He was right in believing that his wife was beside herself. For more than two days, she had been calling around everywhere, including his company headquarters in New York, his family in France (thinking that he had taken an impromptu flight to visit them), and his office in Dubai. No one had a clue as to where he had gone. It was as if he had simply vanished into thin air. After a while, she began to think the worst but would not allow herself to sink into an abyss of fear. She held her children close and took comfort in the company of Sophie, who was always optimistic.

"You know Mr. Bouchard. He likes to travel. He may have just decided to stop off somewhere. At any moment, the phone will ring," Sophie said reassuringly.

Unfortunately for Georgette, however, that didn't happen. Instead, Daniel remained focused on his mission. He continued to comb the streets of Berlin, glancing in coffee shops, boutiques, and music stores in hopes of catching a glimpse of Greta, but sadly, she was nowhere. He pulled out the tattered piece of paper in his pocket on which he had scribbled her address—a location he had committed to memory after writing her so many letters, words unreciprocated, unanswered.

"Frankfurter Allee. I remember," he whispered. He hailed a cab and indicated his destination to the cab driver.

"You're not from here. Is that a French accent that I detect?" the driver inquired.

"Yes, you are right. I am just visiting … from Paris." The badge on Daniel's breast pocket kept slipping down—a cruel reminder of the pretense surrounding his presence in Germany—and he fumbled as he tried to adjust it.

"What brings you here?" The taxi chauffeur continued to probe as if he truly did suspect something suspicious. "These are dangerous times."

"Oh, I'm just looking for someone." Clearly, Daniel was struggling with the language. In an effort to be a tourist and to help himself along, he had written twenty useful phrases on a piece of paper: "Wo ist die nächste Bank?" ("Where is the nearest bank?") "Wo ist der Bahnhof?" ("Where is the train station?") "Ich hätte gerne einen Kaffee, bitte. ("I'd like a coffee, please.") There were others too, but none of these pleasantries served him in the present moment.

Suddenly, shots rang out, and in an instant, the noises surrounded the taxi and the entire area. Then, a sudden lull ensued.

"Make a run for it!" the cab driver demanded. Do you see that building on the right?" he gestured. "Go in there! I have to get out of here!"

"No! Please, wait for me!" Daniel begged him. "I'm in a hurry, and I have to get to Frankfurter Allee right away," he said in very broken German.

"I will wait for five minutes—just *five* minutes. The taxi driver held up his hand. If you don't come out by then, I'm leaving."

Daniel darted out of the cab. Just as he reached the building, a barrage of bullets surrounded him. A faint scream emanated from his throat as he managed to open the door and enter safely. The cab driver waited as an onslaught of firing continued for about three minutes, which seemed like an eternity. Daniel bravely ran from the building as the firing paused.

"Danke schön!" He panted as he entered the cab again, feeling fortunate to be alive.

The ride lasted ten minutes before they reached Greta's home. Daniel's heart raced with anticipation and exhaustion. He paid the fare, wished the cab driver well, and expressed his gratitude. Then, he hurriedly approached some neighbors standing outside the house. Using what little German he had, he stated his purpose. "Ich bin journalist, und ich suche Greta."[13]

Before he could answer, the neighbor said decisively, "Die Familie wohnt hier nicht mehr. Sie haben drei oder vier Jahren das Haus verlassen. Ich weiß nicht wo sie gegangen sind."[14] He shrugged. More questions led to dead ends.

Daniel was crestfallen. *How difficult could it be to find one person? Was his quest too much to ask, and was closure too much of a tall order?* Such were the questions that he pondered as he sauntered off back to the hotel, filled with disappointment.

That evening, after a quick dinner, he hurriedly wrote a note and placed the badge that the gentleman had given him safely inside. He then went to room 203 and slipped both under the door. There wasn't a person in sight. He was safe, but he had come away empty-handed. Still, he was thankful for the good-hearted gentleman's selflessness and trust. "Words cannot express my gratitude. I will never forget your kindness. – Daniel," the note read.

---

[13] "I am a journalist, and I am searching for Greta."

[14] "The family doesn't live here anymore. The left the house three or four years ago. I don't know where."

Back in his room, sleep came swiftly, despite his rambling thoughts about the repercussions awaiting him at home. *I will be calm and offer no excuse. I will just say,* "I am glad to have returned, and a slight detour took longer than I expected. I'm sorry for any concern that I have caused." Daniel rehearsed the words in the mirror. The next day, he packed up and then continued to scour the streets one last time but to no avail. Greta was gone, and he could only imagine where she was, what her life was like, and if, by chance, she had ever thought of him over the years.

What am I doing? Daniel thought to himself. *I am a married man. I must get home to my family. They will be worried and waiting. At dusk, I will be on my way. What will I say, and how will I handle this? We always try to find a solution after the fact, when it's too late.*

On the nearly seven-hour night flight home, Daniel experienced intense anxiety. Nothing could have prepared the beleaguered man for what would occur, how his wife would react, or the long-term effects on their recently restored relationship. It was clear, however, that something would happen that would either maintain or sever their bond. Daniel's heart quickened as he contemplated the unforeseen.

When he arrived home in the early morning, an emotional Georgette rushed into his arms, in tears. "Oh, mon cher, I don't know whether to embrace or pummel you with soft fists." Laughter and tears comingled as she kissed her husband, who stood there silently with a bewildered expression on his tired face.

"Are you all right? Do you have any idea what you put us through— especially me? I called everyone and everywhere, and I practically had the world looking for you. No one knew where you were."

"I'm so sorry, my angel. I took a slight detour that lasted longer than I ever could have expected. I didn't mean to go missing for two nights and three days, but it was ..."

Daniel stammered.

"I nearly called the gendarmes. I was terrified. It's just not like you to disappear like that. I know that you are a free spirit when it comes to travel. You love to explore, the world is your oyster, and you are like a little child in its midst, always seeking ..." Georgette looked distraught.

Little do you know whom I was seeking, Daniel thought, as his heart filled with remorse.

"You are exhausted. Let's go to sleep, and you can tell me all about your adventure in the morning." Georgette's voice and demeanor were the sweetest Daniel had ever known, and her reception only made he feel even more guilty.

The next day was Sunday, and conversation over breakfast was reduced to monosyllables on Daniel's part. Everything that his wife said and every one of her questions was met with a yes or no answer. Seeing that he was burdened, she allowed him to brood in silence. Later, he announced that he would go to the beach with the children for a while and get some fresh air, while she shopped with Sophie.

"Something is wrong with Daniel," she told her confidante. "He is not right. I believe in open communication, but he is furtive, clandestine, and disinclined to share his heart with me. He is a good man, but I cannot help being suspicious. Since he has come home, barely two words have left his mouth. He is hiding something … I feel it!"

"Ah, you know, sometimes men just have to be left to their thoughts. We cannot expect them to reveal everything. The tide will come in. Just keep looking at the moon's light. Where there is love, there is hope." Sophie smiled encouragingly.

"I don't know what I would do without your friendship. Perhaps you are right," Georgette said wistfully.

Over the course of the next twenty-four hours, Daniel's silence persisted, as unrest smoldered within Georgette's heavy heart. The following day when Daniel left for work, she could wait no longer. She had to find answers and uncover the shroud of mystery surrounding her husband's unexplained disappearance, so she sneaked into their room and rummaged through his desk. There, she found his passport stamped for New York and Germany.

Germany? What was he doing there? He never mentioned that to me. Why would he go there without telling me?

Probing further, Georgette found a stack of letters tied with a colorful bow and hidden beneath some contracts and other official documents. One of the letters especially caught her attention, as it emitted a faint fragrance of Daniel's cologne. Slightly trembling, she unfolded the letter and began to read a copy of the last letter Daniel had written to Greta, which he had carefully kept hidden away:

To the Only One Who Fulfilled My Dreams:

Greta, it has been nearly six months since you left and I
first wrote to you, but you have not even sent a brief reply to
explain why you departed. How could you be so dismissive?
I have been trying my best to heal the wounds of my soul,
but until now, without closure, I cannot move on.

Georgette could not read further. Suddenly, her heart began to speak to
her. *He never loved you. He merely seized the moment to capture your attention
and heal from his incomprehensible loss. You are a rebound love, a convenience
meant to shroud the pain that he cannot face. You saw the red flags, but you
didn't pay heed. You told him to show you the world. His charm lured you and
you sought to make him forget, but he has never been able to take his mind off
her. Instead, he continues to try to fill that void. Perhaps, he never will. Now,
you have given your heart. You are all in, but he is absent and aloof. His mind
wanders, his eye roves, and you … You wait for him to change, but he never will.*

That evening, when Daniel came home from work, she confronted him
in no uncertain terms. "Why were you in Germany? Don't deny it. I found
the passport and your last letter to Greta. 'To the Only One Who Fulfilled
My Dreams!' Indeed! You were looking for her, weren't you? Weren't you?"
Georgette repeated in anguish.

Daniel could not avert the truth and barely found the strength to utter
words.

"I want a divorce," Georgette said with controlled anger.

Silence came in reply.

"This marriage is over. It's enough," Georgette continued.

Daniel could not negate her hurt feelings with a response. Nothing he
could say would change her mind.

"I will leave for France tomorrow. I have already called Jean-Paul," she
declared.

Daniel's heart raced. He knew that the strong bond that existed between
the families would be shaken. Fraught with guilt, he still said nothing.

"I am taking the children. I don't want them to be traumatized. I have
simply told them that we are going to visit their grandparents and uncle.
Please don't speak a word to them about anything else."

"Understood," was all Daniel could say.

That evening, he took his belongings and slept in the guest room, while Georgette cried herself to sleep. She wondered what her future would be like, how she could manage without Daniel, and how the magic had so precipitously ended (though she could not say that her world had collapsed without warning). The warning signs were everywhere, but she chose to paint them with a rosy brush. She knew that in his heart, her husband was well-meaning, but she couldn't live in the shadow of another woman's image—even if that relationship had, in fact, ended. She resolved to be calm, breathe deeply, and be strong for the children. In time, the wounds would heal. She had to believe that. The little ones would forge a connection with their father. *Love always finds a way*, she affirmed.

Meanwhile, Daniel lay in the silence of a cold room, feeling numb and alone, with the music of Gheorghe Zamfir and Ottmar Liebert taunting his brain. "I'm sorry, my love," he whispered, hoping that Georgette's spirit would somehow hear his. He too did not know what the future would bring. He just had to move forward.

The next morning, he quietly left for work and went about his day as usual, trying not to think of the emptiness that awaited him in that other world—the life that he and his wife had built together. He had to admit that he somehow knew all along that it would end, through no fault of Georgette's, but rather the fear that haunted him. And now, what he dreaded most had occurred. The situation was a self-fulfilling prophecy.

Upon returning home, Daniel felt an almost eerie quiet, as if the world had abandoned him—or vice versa. His three children and his wife seemed a universe away, out of reach, and his heart wept at the thought. Georgette left a note that he found on the refrigerator door. *I will call you soon. The children love you. Sophie decided to leave with us. It is best this way.*

Kneeling, Daniel began to sob. Then, suddenly, as he regained composure, he noticed that Fifi, the female lovebird, lay very still. Approaching the cage, he stared at Bernard, peering down at her with a fixed gaze. Daniel paused for a while and noticed that Fifi wasn't breathing. He opened the cage and held her gently in his hand. She was gone! Like everything else in his life at that moment, her death was a complete mystery. Overwhelmed with compassion for Bernard, he asked himself, "Am I to remain like this little fellow, imprisoned by sorrow with a woman who no longer can love me, or shall I take a risk and break free?"

In that moment, as happiness seemed to elude him, he suddenly realized that he had to let Bernard take flight and go on his way now that Fifi was no more. Tearfully, he went to the balcony, opened the door, and allowed the bird to fly away. He looked on with pathos, as his star-crossed feathered friend took to the air, embracing freedom. Somehow, Daniel related. For both, love had died, and one heart could not remain stable and dwell in happiness without the other whom it had cherished for so long. With these thoughts in mind, Daniel was determined to search for meaning in his life again—independently. He could not turn back and beg for forgiveness. It was too late for that. Sad and alone, he was ready to fly. *But where?* He had no clue, trapped in his life's cage.

Chapter 19

The Guillotine

The silence that prevailed in the house was deafening. The clamor, noise, and laughter to which he had been so accustomed were mere echoes of the past, and as hard as he tried, Daniel could not quiet that memory. Occasionally, he would find a child's toy on the floor and pick it up as though it were the greatest treasure—only a remnant of what used to be. Deep inside, the brokenhearted husband/father knew that life would resume a semblance of normalcy, but he just did not know how and from where comfort would come. Everywhere he looked, painful memories filled all space, like shadowy ghosts rising up to taunt him. Once again, those who were absent loomed everywhere.

Nighttime was the most difficult challenge of all, the setting sun serving as a cruel reminder that loneliness would be his constant companion. Daniel tried to mask the pain by frequenting bars and drinking every night, coming home, and literally crashing onto his bed, barely able to close his eyes for two or three hours.

One morning, unable to sleep at all, he got into his car and just drove … toward nowhere. On a bridge in Dubai, he felt like he had the road to himself. Not a soul was in sight, except a Range Rover on his right side. All of a sudden, that vehicle disappeared. Daniel looked in the rearview mirror, wondering where it was. *Should I stop?* he asked himself. Then, acknowledging that he was slightly inebriated, he decided to continue on his way. He feared that a police officer would spot him, discover his compromised state, and arrest or fine him. At the time, he was not aware of the tragedy that had befallen the Range Rover's four passengers.

They had been in a horrible accident and had plummeted into the sea. Had he stopped, he could have saved their lives; yet, when he found out about the horrific incident, he did not even feel a tinge of guilt. He was too caught up in the why-me? syndrome to feel for others. This lack of compassion was not part of his nature in any way, but then again, he had lost himself entirely. He was not the man his father and grandmother had raised. Rather, he was dwelling in an alternate consciousness—a cavernous abyss of sorrow that had changed his heart. Later, the tragedy would become almost a fixture in his thoughts, a reminder of one of the greatest omissions in his life.

Despite his alcohol-induced indifference, the days moved on. He and Georgette spoke a few times on the phone; however, she chose to avoid rather than confront him. Soon, she asked for an official divorce, and he promised to travel to France and draw up the papers with his attorney.

Amid the emotional turmoil, he planned to resign from his position and decided to leave for Paris to determine his next career move. Everything— even his most important projects—seemed almost meaningless. He was restless and needed new intellectual challenges.

Soon, he left the marital home and resolved to literally and figuratively close the door on all his memories of that place. A few days before he left the house for an extended-stay hotel, he gathered his belongings and found some undeveloped film in the closet containing images of Georgette and the children at the beach. *Developing the film is one way of preserving the good times*, he thought.

Upon arriving at the local photo store, he met a Korean lady who reassured him that his photos would be ready within a few days, at his request. Handing her his card, he hurried away, feeling a measure of peace. *At least those memories will be enshrined forever*, he told himself. However, with all that he had on his mind, Daniel allowed two weeks to pass without returning phone calls from the store and forgot all about the photos. He was too busy at work to address the issue, so the Korean lady finally took matters into her own hands and dropped off the film at the business address listed on his card. This was an unusual gesture, but after viewing the photos, she felt that they were deeply meaningful to him.

"The gentleman who would have taken care of this is on leave, and I just thought that the photos must be important and I didn't want to wait," she explained. "You have adorable children and a lovely wife."

Daniel swallowed hard and tried not to reveal his emotions. "They are not here now. My wife and I are having … issues," he said tentatively. "I'm going to follow them in the next few months and go to Paris."

There was something so sincere and pleasant in the lady's demeanor that made Daniel feel a strange connection to her. Within the next few days, he found more unexposed film and called to ask if the lady could help.

"Of course," she said, "but don't bother to come to the store. I'm in your area, and I'll pick up the film from you."

"Thank you kindly … Sorry, what is your name?" Daniel replied.

"Mi Jin," the lady said.

"Many thanks again."

The next day, Mi Jin came around lunchtime, and Daniel invited her for a bite at a nearby restaurant. The two conversed and soon struck up a friendship. They talked for more than an hour and instantly felt at ease in one another's company.

By that time, Daniel's life had become more logistically convenient. He had rented his extended-stay hotel suite so that he would not have to worry about housekeeping details, such as laundry and shopping. His primary focus was killing time. Unfortunately, alcohol had become his only true friend, but all of a sudden, Mi Jin's presence gave him renewed hope and purpose, and after speaking with each other every few days, the two decided to meet again at the corner bar, close to his hotel.

There, after a few drinks, Daniel poured out his heart and soul. "My life is characterized by loss—loss of the people I love and love itself. I don't know why, but nothing ever works out. Each time I give my heart, I lose it. Every time I believe in commitment, something happens to destroy it. This has been the story of my life since I was a child." For some reason, he also felt compelled to tell her the story of the birth of his first daughter, Arielle, and how the nurse, Annabelle, had saved her life. "I was so relieved that someone was there who cared when I wasn't present. Somehow, without intending to err, I always make mistakes—either by the wrong timing, the wrong place, or the wrong people. That is why relationships don't come easily to me. I'm always afraid of losing the person I deeply love."

Mi Jin was sympathetic. "Why shouldn't you have someone to love and care for you? Why should you always experience loss? To love you is probably the most natural thing that any woman can feel—even after only a brief time knowing you." She reached over and took Daniel's hand.

Her words moved him, and in a short time, their connection grew and intensified. Soon, they agreed to spend the evening together. For Mi Jin, this was true love. She would never have given her heart under any other condition. She knew that she wanted to spend warm moments with her newfound love interest, but he was (not surprisingly) noncommittal.

In Daniel's mind, he told himself, *For women, physical intimacy is the ultimate sign of love, but for men, such is not always the case. My heart and mind are in so many places that I hardly know who I am anymore. My life is falling apart, and I have nowhere to turn.*

So, while acknowledging Mi Jin's feelings, he decided to back away. "I don't know what will happen in the future," he told her. "I have three children, the state of my marriage is unclear, and I may ultimately move back to New York in the next four to six months."

Mi Jin was left stunned to ponder what had occurred between them, and before she knew what was happening, Daniel had returned to Paris, trying to survey the state of things there. The news was not good. He felt as though he were going to the guillotine—certain death. The executors: his brother and the whole family who, since the breakup, had become increasingly estranged from Georgette's relatives.

"My brother," Pierre began sternly when the two men were together, "I don't know what to say. You have ruined everything. You lost her; she didn't lose you. You have been irresponsible and dismissive of the greatest treasure in your life. I cannot say anymore."

Daniel could not say a word in reply and departed feeling ashamed. Never had such pain welled within him before. Going home had always been a source of comfort and peace, a place for personal reflection and family time. Now, however, the visit generated strife—a constant reminder of his transgressions and how he had let down two families. He just couldn't bear the thought, let alone having to face his brother's anger and disappointment. That was the worst part. His rock and mentor had thrown up his hands.

Like a lost lamb, Daniel went to Georgette's home the following day. As she opened the door, without even saying hello, she declared, "Let me go."

"I didn't know your value," Daniel admitted. "I knew that you loved me so much, and I couldn't match the depth of such love. I'm sorry for everything, and I hope that you will someday find someone who will appreciate and treasure your heart. Please know that you will have whatever financial support that you require."

"Don't worry. I know how to care for my children in every way," Georgette affirmed.

"Just give me time to establish myself in New York. I am going there soon. Once I settle in, we can discuss their future."

Georgette was deeply hurt. "You know, Daniel," she said, "I have supported you in every way possible. I was so happy for you whenever you received your promotions at work. I felt as though that good fortune had happened to me directly." She paused for a moment to reflect and then continued. "My conscience is clear. I gave you all that I had—my heart. Never believe that anyone will go to such lengths as I have for you."

I threw that love away, Daniel said to himself.

Every one of Georgette's words cut like a knife in his heart, because he knew that they resonated with truth. Pierre was right; he had ruined *everything.* He then asked to see the children and presented them with gifts.

"Papa! You are here!" Little Arielle jumped in her father's arms, while Claudette and Jean Pierre timidly clung to their mother's dress, sensing tension in the room.

"It is clear that more than gifts, the children need their father," Georgette stated.

Daniel nodded. *I have made the biggest mistake,* he told himself. *I could not feel guiltier, and this is my emotional guillotine. I cannot stay in Paris. There is too much turmoil here. I must leave and go to New York, where I can have some peace, join my company's headquarters, and rethink my next career move.* Such were the thoughts that swarmed through Daniel's brain. He felt that he had been unfair to everyone who had ever meant anything in his life, and he had to find a way to set himself on track.

Despite his desire for stability, Daniel's heart was torn in a million different directions. While he was struggling to overcome the anguish of his failed marriage (for which he assumed the entire blame), he could not avoid the fact that Mi Jin was a part of his life—at least, that was her fondest intent.

As he finalized the last details before his departure and rummaged through his possessions, Daniel found a necklace that Mi Jin had given him, depicting two halves of a heart with the word *love* inscribed on each. *Into how many halves must I divide my weary heart?* Daniel asked himself. *I have to set my life on course, once and for all. That will only happen if I focus solely on myself, my work, my future, and impending matters concerning my children. I have no time to waste—not anymore—and I am finished with hurting people. I want that part of me to be consigned to the past forever.*

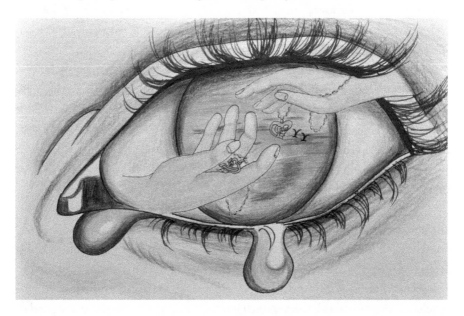

By all appearances, Mi Jin was not going away. Ironically (though unbeknownst to her at the time), she was in the same position in which Daniel found himself when Greta left him. She persisted in letting her feelings show, and the relationship evolved. Soon, she introduced Daniel to her uncle, Jong-Hyun, a prominent physician who instantly saw the connection between them. In private, she said, "I love him, Uncle." Inside, however, she sensed that Daniel's heart was elsewhere.

"Why, Daniel, do you always speak of your wife and never ask about or focus on me? You must still have deep feelings for her. Where do I fit into this equation?" she would ask.

Daniel barely knew where *he* stood, let alone how to compartmentalize his affections and emotions. For about a week, he returned to Dubai, where he gathered his belongings and shipped them to New York.

"Hopefully, I will be there for only a couple of months, and then I will send for you," he promised.

Mi Jin was inwardly distressed but graciously offered her support. "Whatever is best for you to do, I endorse," she said. "Your happiness is my own."

Within a couple of weeks, Daniel went to the airport and prepared to fly to New York. At the terminal, Mi Jin bid him farewell with tears in her eyes. She truly loved him, and just then, at that very moment, he also thought, *She is the one with whom I can spend the rest of my life—or at least, she is the one at hand now, for this moment.*

Upon his arrival, Daniel felt that he had literally and figuratively landed into a more settled future. He was exhausted and eager to relax and enjoy his company-sponsored apartment on the Upper West Side of New York City. After one night's rest, he committed himself entirely to his work, immersing himself in projects—all with the intent of forgetting his pain. Mi Jin called twice and left messages, but he was too self-absorbed and focused on the details of his job to respond.

Two months elapsed before he returned Mi Jin's calls, and by then, she was nowhere to be found. Her number had been disconnected. Nearly frantic with worry and guilt, he called her workplace and even asked a friend to try to locate her. He soon discovered that she had not returned to the store in at least a month. Her uncle was on vacation and could not be reached but returned about a month later. At that time, Daniel attempted to call him again at the hospital where he worked. This time, he was successful.

"Do you know where Mi Jin has gone? I cannot find her anywhere," he began.

"She doesn't want to see you," Jong-Hyun said candidly.

"I appreciate your honesty. I have been so worried. I thought that something happened to her. I'm so sorry and sad that she feels that way, but at least I know that she is all right," Daniel replied, trying to conceal his humiliation.

Where could she have gone? Have I lost, yet again? Must life be filled with so much anguish? Not only have I experienced pain, but I, myself, am lost. There must be an answer, and I must find it! Daniel cried silently, as if in supplication.

That night, after searching for Mi Jin in vain, he lay down on his bed and closed his eyes—not to sleep, but in a desperate attempt to shield himself from the world.

Chapter 20

The Sacrifice

Dear Diary,

A year has passed since Georgette and I parted ways, and I have not lived with my children. To say that circumstances have been challenging is an understatement. One day flows into the next like molasses being poured into a jar. I take joy in very little, and I mask my pain and sorrow with alcohol. I realize that drinking solves nothing, only serving as a means of escape for me, but I resolve to stop—today. I have to make some very serious decisions about myself and my children's future. I acknowledge that up until now, I have not been a real father to them. Parenting involves so much more than a biological connection. I want to be here for them, protect them, show them how much I love them, and prove to them that I can be much more than a father who tells bedtime stories.

I have hurt more people than I care to admit—even to myself—but such was never my intention. I also have been on the receiving end of the pain, but now I know that it's

not all about me. The only thing that matters is the well-
being of my kids.

Upon writing these words, Daniel had an epiphany: he would go to
France and speak with Georgette about raising the children. This was a
huge step, but he wanted to meet his obligations to the fullest extent. For
three days, he took a leave from multiple projects, assigning them to his
trusted assistant.

He called Georgette but didn't say a word about his ultimate intention.
Instead, he merely stated, "We must talk about a crucial matter."

Georgette was intuitive, and sensing what the issue was, she replied, "I
am staying with my family, but I will meet you at a nearby café, and we can
speak about the children." She was very stoic and firm, but the underlying
kindness and patience in her tone touched his heart. He felt undeserving
but grateful and filled with hope.

Soon, however, Daniel's nerves got the best of him, and he almost
phoned at the last minute to cancel, but he finally took the plunge and
allowed nothing to hold him back. Within a week after he made his decision
to travel to France, he was on a plane. He slept the whole way and tried not
to let his mind ramble. Most of all, he was determined not to visit his family
or inform them of his plans. As much as he cherished their input on all
matters, he felt that this situation was an exception. Their minds were too
clouded with judgments and disappointments, which would undoubtedly
obstruct his ultimate objective.

Upon meeting with Georgette, he complimented her on her appearance.
"You are more beautiful than ever," he said.

"Thank you," she replied, lowering her eyes, so as not to meet with
Daniel's. "I hope that you are well. The girls miss you terribly, and even little
Jean Pierre is now saying *Papa*."

Daniel was deeply touched. "That's why I need them."

"What do you mean?" Georgette looked puzzled.

"I want to raise them, Georgette. I want to be their father, to see them
grow up, and to show them love as I never have before. I want the chance to
be the father I never was."

Georgette remained silent for a moment. "But how can you raise three
children when you cannot properly care for yourself? I don't mean any

disrespect, and I'm sure that you know what I am saying. You are working all the time, and you have your friends, your parties, and your nightlife. How will you be able to shoulder such a huge responsibility? How can you change overnight?"

"Your questions are very wise and appropriate, but I will manage," Daniel said quietly. "I promise that I will do right by them. They will be more than well cared for, and I will live up to my responsibilities like the proud and grateful father they deserve."

"Apparently, you have thought this through extensively, or you would not have come all this way to communicate with me." Georgette now fixed her eyes on her estranged husband.

"Again, you are perfectly right," Daniel admitted. "I am entirely serious, and I will not disappoint you or them."

Georgette saw and felt the earnestness and sincerity in Daniel's voice. "Well, then, if this is your decision, I will go along with it, as long as I can also be in their lives and visit at any time. They are my life."

"That goes without saying. I would not have things any other way."

"You are a puzzlement, Daniel Bouchard, but I know that your heart is in the right place. If this is what you want to do, knowing how much you love our children, I will go along with you. In a couple of weeks, I will take them to New York and stay with you in your guest room for two weeks to see them through the transition. This may be very difficult, but I will try my best to acclimate them to the new living arrangement and reassure them of my love and constant presence in their lives."

"I know that you will. I won't have you stay in the guest room. That will be my place for two weeks. I will prepare my room for you, and I will be the guest." Daniel smiled.

"Thank you." Georgette looked solemn. "You must remember that this is not about us. We have to make sure that our children are comfortable. As painful as this past couple of years have been for us, we cannot compare what we have endured to our children's adjustments. They are very strong, and they will be fine."

As the devoted mother spoke, her eyes filled with tears. The two stayed together until the dinner hour and talked about many details that would, potentially, affect the whole family. They agreed not to involve their respective siblings or Georgette's parents, who would object to the arrangement. Clashes of personalities and opinions would, undoubtedly, be the order of the day, and they wanted to make conditions as easy and trauma-free as possible for the children.

Feeling emotionally satiated, Daniel returned home and prepared for his family's arrival. Georgette's humanity and selflessness truly overwhelmed him. *She must love me very much to make this sacrifice*, he told himself. *I truly am an extremely fortunate man.*

The days passed quickly, and finally, the moment arrived for Daniel to meet Georgette and the children at Kennedy Airport in New York City. At their first glimpse of their father, the girls practically flew into his arms, especially Arielle, who had composed a special song for him, *Papa Ours, je'taime!* Daniel cried tears of joy upon seeing them, and so did Jean Pierre, though his tears stemmed more from bewilderment than happiness.

Upon their arrival at Daniel's upscale New York apartment, Georgette remarked, "This is quite impressive—a monument to your success."

"Yes, I am happy here, but something is definitely missing—or, I should say, three *someones*." Daniel smiled with a tinge of melancholy, adding, "Not anymore." He gestured to embrace his former wife in a friendly manner.

She recoiled. "Please show me to my room," she said. "We will be fine here for two weeks until you make other arrangements when ..." she caught herself, not wanting to reveal their plans to the children.

"Are we going to live in this grand building now, Mama?" Arielle wanted to know.

"I will let you know, darling," Georgette answered evasively.

Georgette spent her days sightseeing with the girls, while she left Jean Pierre with a sitter for a few hours. She toured the Statue of Liberty, the Metropolitan Museum of Art, the Central Park Zoo, and the new Freedom Tower.

The girls were inspired and continuously declared, "Yes, Mama! We should live here."

When the two-week stay was coming to an end, Arielle posed her question again. At nearly five, she was a precocious child, intensely curious, and filled with wonderment about everything. "Mama, you said to me, 'I will let you know.' Tell me, is this our home now?"

"My angel, yes. I have something to tell you." Georgette took her oldest daughter in her arms. "You will live with Papa now."

At first, Arielle didn't understand. "Hooray! We will be together, all of us together again!"

"No, sweetheart. Not me. Just you, Claudette, and Jean Pierre. Papa loves you so much that he wants you to live with him. I will come and visit you all the time, and we can speak on the telephone every day."

"But, Mama, you will not be here with us every day?" Arielle asked tearfully.

"No, dearest one. I will not be here, but I will be in your heart, and I will come to see you often. If you need me here, I will fly to you. You know that I will. Do you know how much I love you? Do you know how much you mean to me?"

Arielle nodded, and Claudette appeared from behind, having listened to the whole conversation. As the girls clung to her neck, Georgette was on the verge of tears, but like the selfless, gracious woman she was, she never displayed the depth of her emotions. *I must be very strong for them,* she said to herself.

"As you wish, Mama," Arielle said with resignation far beyond her years.

"As you wish, Mama," Claudette parroted, unsure of what she had agreed to.

"These are my girls, my treasures! Will you promise me that you will look after your little brother?"

"Yes!" both girls said in unison.

Now that the excruciating task of telling them is over, I must leave soon. I do not want to prolong the agony. I must return to France and my family. I will tell them that the kids are staying with Daniel for just a little while. That will discourage their questions and protestations. Such were Georgette's thoughts, as she went to pack.

"Are you leaving so soon? You have barely been here two weeks. You are more than welcome to stay, you know," Daniel began.

"Thank you, but no. My life is in France, and my family is waiting. I must go to them and leave the children to begin their life here with you."

"I understand," he replied. "I want to thank you for everything that you have done for me—for all of the sacrifices that you have made for my sake."

"Just be a good father to our children. That's all the thanks I need."

"I will take you to the airport tomorrow."

And so, the next day, Georgette prepared to leave, while a babysitter watched the children. They were astonishingly resigned to what was happening and bid their mother farewell without a tear.

"Please come back soon, Mama, please!" Arielle urged. "Wave to Mama, Jean Pierre," she said, holding her little brother in her arms.

"I cannot wait!" the angelic mother replied, trying to put on her brightest smile—a beautiful mask of all that she felt within her heart.

When Daniel left her off at the airport, the devoted mother gestured a sweet, cordial wave of the hand in his direction. In that moment, more than ever, Daniel understood all that he had lost—and how much he had gained—all in an instant.

Chapter 21

The Unexpected

The process of taking in his three beloved children not only signified becoming a father to Daniel; it was also a time of self-discovery, personal accountability, and essentially, raising himself. He fell into a methodical routine with the girls and little Jean Pierre, rising at seven thirty every morning and returning home at five o'clock each evening. In the interim, he hired an all-day sitter for the little boy, while Arielle and Claudette attended the same school. They delighted in being together, learning English and a variety of other subjects. When he came home from work, Daniel was prepared to answer a thousand questions, help with homework, and make sure the children were well nourished. He also learned the all-important lesson that he could no longer be the center of his own universe. There were other precious lives he had to gently orchestrate, and he rose to the occasion with a willing and grateful heart. For the first time in more than three decades, his home was filled with the joy of laughter, running, playing, and other noisy engagement that made him forget all of his past mistakes and misgivings. He played with the children's toys, read bedtime stories, and acted out like a child himself, all to their delight and amusement.

The girls acclimated beautifully, taking turns bringing plates to the table at mealtime, washing dishes, and being little mothers to their baby brother. This type of structure gave them a sense of purpose and belonging, and although they missed their mother tremendously, they knew she could be there at a moment's notice. Distance meant absolutely nothing where love was concerned.

Georgette visited once every two to three months and stayed for a week or two with the children. Once again, Daniel took the guest room where he could retreat, so as not to interfere with Georgette's special bonding time. He respected the strong, indelible connection between mother and children and refrained from emotional attachment to Georgette. He held fast to his firm belief that you cannot mend a broken vase and analogized his failed relationships and love connections to fragile, damaged objects that could never be restored. What truly mattered was the beautiful relationship that he had cultivated with his children. These were his life's golden years, free of mistakes and regrets.

In fact, Daniel himself was growing up, courtesy of his children's guidance and needs. He met every responsibility with amazing aptitude and joy, never wishing to be anywhere else or with anyone else. They were his all and completely fulfilled him. He was so proud and overjoyed that he had manifested his destiny as a father and was able to raise them with smiles on their faces, grounded and content.

Of course, each time the girl's asked, "Papa, why can't Mama live with us?" his heart was torn in two.

"We cannot live together, my darlings. It's not easy to understand, but when you grow up, you will." The girls were so mature and brave about the matter and served as an example to their father, gracefully accepting their parents' decision to remain apart.

As they grew, the girls began to help Daniel around the house with cleaning, cooking, and running errands. Each day, they emulated their mother more and more and remained very close to each other. Their dad came to call them the twins. Jean Pierre was quickly growing as well and was a little prince to his sisters, who doted on him at every turn. Their mother was intensely proud that she had been with all of them during their formative years and had raised such responsible, beautiful children. Now it was Daniel's turn—and their opportunity, in their own way—to raise *him*.

One of the things that he and his children loved most was to travel together to visit family in Paris. Pierre and Adelle were extremely anxious to see the girls and little Jean Pierre, as were their cousins, Amélia and Jacques, especially at Christmastime. The trip would also give the children a much-desired opportunity to visit their mother and spend time with their maternal family as well. On school break one Christmas, the girls clamored to pack for themselves and their little brother and even carted their father's suitcase to the car.

"We took more for you, Papa!" they exclaimed.

"Did you take the kitchen sink too? Why do I need all of those belongings?"

"Well, you never know," Arielle said in her most maternal tone.

Daniel felt truly blessed. He was also a little anxious about seeing his brother again, realizing that he had disappointed him and estranged him from Georgette's family. Once best friends, Jean-Paul and Pierre could barely look at one another without feeling a measure of heartache and bitterness.

Once at home in Paris, however, Daniel and his three angels, as he called his children, were received with the utmost love and joy.

"Will you stay for a while?" Pierre asked, looking slightly older, but intensely distinguished in a beard.

"Two weeks, Brother, if you will have me," Daniel said, looking down.

"If I will have you? You are part of me. Why are you so solemn?" Pierre asked.

"Well, you know what transpired. You said yourself that I ruined everything."

"Let that be water under the bridge, Brother. What's done is done. We have to move on with our lives and look out for the children's best interests."

Daniel was grateful for his brother's power of forgiveness, though it did not surprise him. As he looked around, the house was as he remembered it to be when Grand-mère presided over it. Somehow, her presence still seemed to pervade the place, like a benevolent apparition watching over her family.

After the family opened their Christmas gifts and sang carols, with Marie and Collette leading the way at the piano, Daniel announced that he would go to Grand-mère's and Papa's graves to pay his respects. This time, the girls came with him, while little Jean Pierre, still too young to understand the implications of mourning and ritual, stayed at home with the family and played with the many toys that Père Noël[15] had left for him on Christmas Eve.

---

[15] Santa Claus.

126

At the cemetery, the girls held their father's hand as he stood over the graves. This time, instead of deep reflection and grief, Daniel felt a measure of inner peace and reassurance that his beloved father and guardian grandmother were proud of the father he had become.

"The kids have raised me well," he said aloud, holding Claudette gently in his arms. She kissed one of the two roses her father presented to her before placing it on Grand-mère's grave, and then Arielle did the same. The ritual was repeated at Papa's site. The golden ray of light that usually appeared before Daniel's eyes was not there this time, and in his mind, its absence seemed to signal that no further signs from heaven were necessary. Amélia's grandson had all that his heart could ever desire.

Upon their return to the house, Daniel received a call from Georgette, stating that a second Christmas was awaiting the children at her family's home.

"Of course. We will be right there," Daniel said cordially.

Georgette's parents greeted the four warmly and embraced the three children with tears in their eyes. Daniel saw this as his cue to leave, but before he did, he approached his former wife. "If you want to keep them here longer, you are more than free to do so. You can either bring them to New York, or I will return and pick them up. It's your choice."

"I never had a choice," Georgette murmured.

"What did you say? Sorry, I couldn't hear you," Daniel answered.

"It's nothing," Georgette said in a melancholy tone.

Ultimately, the two decided that the children would stay with their mother through the New Year, while their father returned to New York. After two weeks, he came back to retrieve them, observing their glowing complexions, sparkling eyes, and endless stories and recollections that they had to recount about their wonderful vacation with Mama.

Time took flight, and soon, it was 2003. The girls were in high school, off on their break. Their brother, a once bouncing little boy, was in junior high. All impressed their teachers with their many aptitudes and interests. The girls remained extraordinarily close and tended to their little brother as if they had brought him into the world. Together, the three assumed more responsibilities around that time, had structured routines, and were real companions and gifts to their father, whose life was enriched by their presence. In fact, he could never recall a time when he wasn't their father.

They were his purpose and his destiny. He too had reached the end stages of growing pains, both emotionally and psychologically, though he still harbored some deep personal regrets. One of the most prominent of these was the fact that he still had an unresolved communication issue with Mi Jin, the woman with the beautiful smile with whom he had spent one passionate night. Once again, the lack of closure weighed heavily on his mind, and he had no idea where she was … but he was about to find out.

Although his work was going well, Daniel's company branch in Dubai was on the verge of bankruptcy, and he was called in to try to rescue it from almost certain disaster. While there, he wanted to finally discover what had happened to Mi Jin, his lady-love of so long ago with whom he had lost contact. The first thing on his mind, however, was the well-being of his children, and he appealed to their mother to stay with them while he was away for about one month. Georgette readily obliged, returned to New York, and was all too happy to embrace the three angels at every opportunity.

By then, Claudette was a freshman in high school, and her sister Arielle was entering her junior year. In acknowledgment of her superior academic achievements and since she had passed her driver's test on the first try, Arielle's father purchased a jeep for her—an offering that delighted her to no end.

"Papa!" she cried ecstatically. "I don't know what to say."

"Say that you will be careful and enjoy your new wheels, my darling," Daniel replied, tenderly embracing his daughter.

Arielle agreed and promised that she would be more than responsible.

Two days later, Daniel flew to Dubai, promising to call at every opportunity. Once he landed, he took time to relax and decompose, instinctively reverting to his old Gheorghe Zamfir tapes, with a couple of pieces by André Rieu mixed in. Suddenly, in the midst of meditation, Daniel had a thought. *I must call Jong-Hyun, Mi Jin's uncle, the physician. Perhaps, he can tell me her whereabouts.*

As he scrambled among his personal papers to find the number, Daniel wondered whether he still had the correct contact information. It had been more than a decade since he had last communicated with Mi Jin and her uncle, and he was uncertain as to whether he would ever be able to regain contact with either of them. Mi Jin's complete disappearance had left him without a definitive method for finding her. Fortunately, however, when he dialed the number, the voice on the other end of the line sounded familiar. It was, in fact, Jong-Hyun.

"I'm calling to inquire about Mi Jin," Daniel began. "I understand that many years have elapsed, but she has not left my mind. There are many things that I still must explain."

"A long time ago I received strict orders not to speak to you about her," Jong-Hyun said sternly.

"Please, you must tell me where she is now. Enough time has gone by, and I'm still so worried. I have tried several times to reach her without success. There was some miscommunication between us. I believe that she mistakenly thought I abandoned her, but I was so caught up in my work that I hardly knew whether it was day or night and—"

"Listen, Daniel. Come and meet me at the hospital. I have something to tell you that we should address in person."

Jong-Hyun's tone sent chills up and down Daniel's spine. *At the hospital? What could he mean? What has happened?* His mind raced. "Okay. I will be there tomorrow by noon," he said, feeling somewhat uneasy.

A sleepless night followed the conversation, and Daniel could not seem to quiet his restless heart. A flood of questions came pouring into his mind, along with dread that something dire had happened to dear Mi Jin—yet another burden on his already trouble-laden mind. Just when he thought that his life was on an even keel, he was about to be derailed by the unexpected—in more ways than one.

The dawn came crashing through Daniel's window, with a light more blazing and piercing than usual—a metaphor for how he was feeling and a searing reminder that the news he was about to receive would impact him forever. By now, he was used to sudden change and trauma, but he could not help feeling almost sick to his stomach at the mere thought of seeing Jong-Hyun and hearing what he had to say. When he met him at the hospital, he was greeted with calm civility.

"You know," the concerned uncle began. "I was—and remain—under strict orders from Mi Jin not to provide exact information on her whereabouts. She doesn't want to speak to or associate with you. She has had a very traumatic time since you left."

"Please tell me," Daniel said in a beseeching tone. "Is she all right?"

"Now she is, but after you left, she was in a state of emotional turmoil."

"I'm so sorry. You see, I meant to call, but my work—"

Jong-Hyun held up his hand. Please allow me to continue, and then I will hear you out—even though my niece would not want me to do so."

"By all means, please go ahead," Daniel answered as his heart nearly beat out of his chest.

"My niece thought that you would return, as promised, but her calls went unanswered, and as she sank into depression, she decided to close the door on your relationship. She gave you her heart and—"

Daniel gestured to speak, but the protective uncle restrained him and continued.

"You had a night together, she told me. About two months later, she began to feel unwell and went to her primary care physician for a physical. Then and there, at her first checkup, the doctor discovered she was pregnant."

Daniel gasped and staggered slightly. Jong-Hyun beckoned him to sit down and gave him a glass of water.

"Calm yourself. You wanted to know what happened, and now you have to face it."

Daniel nodded.

"As I was saying, once the doctor made that discovery, he asked for a marriage certificate and a declaration of the unborn child's paternal surname. Mi Jin panicked, as she was unmarried and feared that she would succumb to the regulations regarding expectant unwed mothers."

"I'm afraid that I don't know what you are talking about," Daniel said, feeling dazed.

"Here in the United Arab Emirates, there are very stringent regulations regarding unwed expectant mothers. If the woman goes for her first checkup, discovers that she is with child, and is unmarried or does not anticipate being married by a certain date, she is arrested, taken to a kind of shelter (a fancy type of prison), and must expatriate."

"Oh my God! What happens to the child?" Daniel asked in disbelief.

"The child becomes a ward of the state," Jong-Hyun explained.

"I will not allow it! Do you hear me?" Daniel began to rant and become incoherent.

"Please sit down," the physician instructed sternly. "What's done is done."

Daniel hearkened back to when those words recently fell from his brother's lips. Apparently, his mistakes met with no other solution but resignation, but how could he just accept such circumstances?

"Where is my child? Was the baby a boy or a girl? It has been almost ten years. I must find—"

"If you don't calm down, I will have to remove you from the premises. Now, please ... Let me tell you what transpired—uninterrupted."

"Yes, sir," Daniel said, trying to catch his breath.

"The child is a girl. Her name is Annabelle."

Once again, Daniel gasped.

"She is ten years old. When she began to show the pregnancy, Mi Jin drove with a friend to Oman in order to avoid the onslaught of questions that would otherwise await her. That drive lasted twenty hours. She then flew from Muscat Airport back home to Korea, where she had the baby and raised her as a single mother. Understandably, she could not bear to be separated from her—not under any condition. As you know, abortion is illegal here in the UAE, and in all events, Mi Jin abhors that option and would never have considered it. The child is beautiful, healthy, and happy."

"Have ... you ... seen ... her?" Daniel stammered.

"Of course I have seen my granddaughter. Both mother and daughter are doing well. I will revisit them in the New Year."

"Can you please tell them—"

"No. As I said, Mi Jin wants nothing to do with you. I know those are painful words for you to hear, and I'm sorry, but my niece has had her share of distress, and she was fearless to endure the pregnancy and birth without the support of a partner."

Waves of guilt began to wash over Daniel. In that moment, all of his memories came flooding back: feelings of abandonment when his beloved Papa and Grand-mère passed away, his regret over his star-crossed love affair with Greta, his remorse at not being there for Georgette when she gave birth the first time, having an intimate relationship with his secretary during his marriage, and now *this*! It was all too much, and yet, in his heart, he somehow felt that these were fitting penalties for his transgressions. What he failed to acknowledge was that at the core, he was truly good—a work in progress, subject to life's alterations, and no different than anyone else.

Chapter 22

Reappearance of the Rose

If only Daniel could tell his truth to everyone and make them understand his perspective, they would see that he was always at the mercy of circumstance—abandoned and love-deprived in one sense or another. It was not that he victimized himself, but that life itself had dealt him unmanageable hands at times. It seemed that every time he tried to pick himself up out of the mire of guilt and shame, he found himself immersed it in once more, helplessly floundering in emotional quicksand.

What would be appropriate to tell the girls? I'll say ... nothing. Yes, that's it. What they don't know now cannot hurt them, and the last thing I want to do is burden my angels with my indiscreet choices and mistakes. Perhaps, someday, I will find their sister, Annabelle, and introduce them to one another, but that will only occur if I can find her first and if Mi Jin allows me into her life. Oh, what am I thinking? This is all happening too quickly, and I cannot focus. My mind is a maze of confusion, and I must now acknowledge and process the fact that there is a girl in East Asia who deserves to know that she has a biological father somewhere in the world. Somehow, I will find a way ...

Immersed in these thoughts, Daniel closed his eyes and meditated on all of the goodness in his life—above all, his children. Despite all that had transpired with Jong-Hyun and the news that he not only had three, but *four* children (one of whom he might never meet), things began to settle over him like a light mist after a downpour, leaving the hint of more impending rain, but at least, the storm had passed.

The next morning, Daniel had to make a presentation via video conferencing to his company's CEO in New York. The branch had a severe money-collection issue, which caused enormous delays in salary payments and other financial obstacles. If the company could not get back on track, a legal team would have to take over. As he pondered this possibility, Daniel tried to close his eyes and allow his mind to wander.

At the first hint of daylight, he awakened with surprising energy, drove to his office, bounded out of his car, went in, and turned on his computer.

"Good morning, Mr. Bouchard. We are all waiting for you."

Daniel greeted the CEO and staff and began to present his proposals. About ten minutes into the meeting, someone from the HR knocked, opened the door, and told him that there was an urgent phone call for him from New York. Daniel quickly stood, excused himself, and hurried out of the room. The HR receptionist took him aside and handed him the telephone with a concerned expression.

Daniel took the phone and heard Claudette's soft voice. "Papa, Arielle is fine, but she was in a car accident. She broke her leg, and she's in some pain, but she's all right. If there is any more news to report, I will call you immediately. We are at East Side Hospital's emergency room now, but she will be called into a private room soon. I love you! Don't worry."

"My baby girl!" Flashbacks of his losing his father and grandmother in car accidents deluged his mind. His heart raced, and he became frantic. "I need to see her!" Daniel exclaimed. "I will catch the first flight out. Tell her that I will be there soon and I love her."

"Of Course, Papa! Fly safely! Je'taime!"

Daniel sprinted back into his office. "I'm sorry," he said, addressing the CEO. I have a family emergency, and I must leave. I will have to continue the conference in person when I arrive in New York—after this crisis is resolved."

"Please attend to your issue," the CEO said empathetically, "and let us know if you need anything."

"I deeply appreciate your concern, but I don't know anything yet. I will keep you posted as developments arise."

No sooner did he speak these words than Daniel had booked an emergency flight and was driving, in all haste, to the airport. On his way, he wanted to dart every stop sign and jump every red light that he encountered, but something told him not to be reckless. *I'm no longer that twelve-year-old boy alone in the world without my parents, or the boy whose world ended when his grandmother died. I am a father now, and I must own up to my responsibilities by giving rather than receiving, fulfilling expectations instead of anticipating, and understanding rather than wishing to be understood. I only hope that my girl is all right. My children are my life, and I must be there for them in all circumstances.*

With these affirmations firmly set in his heart, the concerned father entered the terminal and boarded his flight. It was noon, and he was scheduled to arrive at about five o'clock that evening (given the difference in time zones) with ample time for visiting his daughter. Once at New York's Kennedy Airport, he hailed a cab.

"East Side Hospital please!" Daniel announced.

In less than fifteen minutes, he arrived at the hospital emergency room, quickening his pace with every step. "I'm Daniel Bouchard. I'm here to see my daughter, Arielle," he told a staff member at the front desk in the waiting room.

"Room 612, sir," came the reply.

Suddenly, in his haste, he bumped into a handsome boy of his daughter's age, approaching and extending his hand.

"Are you Mr. Bouchard?" The young man had a decided European accent.

Daniel nodded in bewilderment.

"I'm Hans, the driver who accidentally collided with your daughter's car. I am a conscientious driver, but for some reason, I lost control of the breaks, and before I realized what was happening, I plowed into your daughter's vehicle. I'm so sorry, sir! Fortunately, she is fine, and I came out without a scratch. I should have done something to avoid her car, but everything happened so quickly, and I take full responsibility for this terrible event."

"I'm in a hurry right now, and I don't have time to speak with you. I'm rushing to see my daughter. Stay here. Don't go anywhere. I'll return to you shortly," Daniel replied imperatively. He was not thinking quite clearly, and the circumstances affected his usual amiable mood.

The boy nodded politely and said that he would see him upstairs. Daniel was then directed to room 612, where his beloved daughter had been transferred. She looked as lovely as ever, but was clearly in distress, with her leg in traction.

"I'm so sorry, Papa. I totaled the car," Arielle said tearfully as soon as she saw her father. "I know that I promised to be careful, and I really tried, but—"

"Please, my angel," Daniel interrupted, "the car means nothing. What I care about is *you*—nothing and no one else. Material possessions can be replaced, but nothing can substitute for the well-being of my angel. You must know that. How are you? How did this happen?" Daniel wanted to know, unable to contain his barrage of questions.

"Well, I was going to the library, just a couple of blocks away. I had just come off the Fifty-Ninth Street Bridge and drove a few blocks when I was broadsided by another vehicle. My car spun around four times and nearly flipped over, but luckily, I was fine—except for my left leg, which hurts so badly," Arielle explained.

"As long as you are all right. That's all that matters. Someday, you will understand that the pain you have now will pale in comparison to other forms of distress you will experience in life, and through it all, I am here for you," the doting papa said tenderly.

Claudette came in and lovingly covered her sister with a blanket and then embraced her father. "Mama was here earlier. She was so worried, but when she saw that Arielle was not severely injured, she felt so relieved."

"You know that her children are everything to her, mon ami," Daniel remarked. "Oh, by the way," he continued. "There is a boy downstairs in the waiting room. Please go there and escort him up. He wants to speak with Arielle."

Claudette went downstairs, and in a few minutes, she reentered the room, accompanied by the young man whom Daniel had recently met.

Claudette leaned over and whispered in her sister's ear. "This boy is gorgeous. You're so lucky that he hit you—I mean, it was fate. You were hit by an angel, someone exceptional, a nonhuman, not like us mere mortals. I wish that he had hit me instead. I'd love to be in your place right now," the younger sibling teased with an impish twinkle in her eyes.

"You wild child. Watch yourself." Arielle whispered, elbowing her back and smiling as Hans looked at her admiringly. "This is my father, Daniel," she said, gesturing.

"What's going on? What are you two talking about?" Daniel asked.

"Oh, it's nothing!" Claudette said dismissively.

"I truly am so sorry, Mr. Bouchard. I never meant to harm your beautiful daughter," Hans repeated.

"You need not apologize to me, but rather, to the young lady who finds herself in this condition on your account," Daniel said sternly.

Then, as the two began to talk, Hans ingratiated himself more. "The police have taken my insurance information, so all costs are covered, and if there is anything I can do to help out, please let me know. My parents have an extra car, and I will be more than happy to drive Arielle around anytime," Hans offered.

"Here is my business card. Please stop by the house at your convenience. I'm sure that my daughter will be happy to see you." Daniel took his leave, impressed by the boy's mannerisms.

Arielle remained in the hospital for two more days before returning home. She had to nurse her injury for two weeks with her leg in a cast. Youth was on her side, however, and she would not have to convalesce for too long. In fact, by the time she arrived home, she was able to use crutches and slightly bear weight on her injured leg. She wasted no time in resuming her household chores. "I cannot let you do things around here entirely alone. This is my duty," she told her papa lovingly.

On her third day at home, Daniel told Georgette that because Arielle was healing, she could return home to France. The family had been deeply concerned and would wish to see their daughter with a smile on her face, relieved and content. Georgette agreed to leave, with a promise to return within the next two weeks for the removal of her daughter's cast.

Daniel drove her to JFK Airport, cordially thanking her, but refraining from any demonstrations of affection. Still, he could not deny that he felt a great deal for her. After all, she was the mother of his children, and she had been blameless for their marriage's dissolution. Daniel resigned himself to the fact that at least, they could be civil to one another and maintain mutual interest in the children's welfare.

"Take good care of her," Georgette said.

"Do you ever doubt that?" Daniel smiled reassuringly.

"That is one thing of which I can be certain," Georgette answered as she turned to enter the terminal.

On the afternoon following Georgette's departure, Hans came to the house to visit Arielle and was permitted to enter her room. The two were very coy, but seemingly reserved with one another, yet the attraction between them was undeniable. Hans seemed honorable and well mannered—the product of a strict but loving upbringing. Daniel grew fonder and fonder of him and permitted the two to remain in Arielle's room with the door open. Hans had brought some flowers and chocolates as a peace offering, which moved Arielle deeply. His kind eyes not only spoke of friendship, but of deep respect and remorse.

The two spent three hours together before Hans looked at his watch. "I had better return home. My parents will worry. If I may, I will come back tomorrow to check in on you."

Just then, Arielle heard Daniel's footsteps on the stairs, and soon, her father entered the room. Immediately, Hans stepped forward to greet him. "Mr. Bouchard, it's good to see you. I'm sorry, but I must go, but Arielle permitted me to return tomorrow. Is there anything I can bring her?"

"Thank you so much. Let me think." Daniel paused. "Well, since she was going to the library when you tried to kill her, and since she can't go right now, as usual, you might want to bring her an interesting book to read," he said with a smile.

Hans and Arielle laughed.

"I have an idea," Hans said. "My mother has a wonderful library at home, and I know just the book that would make your daughter happy." He looked tenderly at Arielle.

The next day, he returned with a book in hand and a tray of cookies for the family. "My mom baked these especially for all of you. I hope that you like them," Hans said politely.

Then, he quickly headed upstairs to Arielle's room, where she awaited him. "I want you to hear my playlist," she offered.

"I'd love to hear!" Hans replied.

Arielle then showed him a family photo album, and the two amused themselves for hours, sharing stories and memories. Clearly, their friendship was evolving.

When it came time to leave, Hans said, "I hope that you like the book. It's quite popular here and in Europe as well."

"A book? Ah, let me see!" Daniel said as he overheard the conversation and entered the room.

"Hans is so sweet," Arielle replied, blushing. "He gave me a book by Heinrich Heine, the nineteenth-century German poet. *Buch der Lieder (Book of Songs)* is very well known. I especially like the one called "Allnächtlich im Traume" ("Nightly in Dreams"). As Arielle reached for the book, it fell to the floor, revealing a single dried rose inside the page containing the poem.

Daniel gasped and closed the book immediately.

Arielle observed that her father's face contorted in agony. "Papa! What's wrong? Please talk to me." By now, she was in tears.

Hans gestured to speak, but Daniel silenced him. "Thank you very much for coming," he said coldly. "We really appreciate it, and now your mission is done. You must not see each other anymore."

"Papa, you are dazed and incoherent. What's wrong with you? You are not rational. You are not yourself."

"Please, sir, if I have done something wrong, tell me," Hans began, turning red and looking very embarrassed and hurt.

"What I said is final. There is nothing to add," Daniel replied with another icy glance. "You must not see one another again. Don't ask questions. Just listen to what I'm telling you. Do you understand me?" Daniel's voice escalated.

Hans swiftly exited the room, ran downstairs, and left out the front door.

Arielle shook her head in disbelief. "I don't understand, Papa. You are suddenly cruel and harsh. For the first time in my life, I don't understand *you*."

"Someday you will," Daniel whispered almost inaudibly.

"Now I know what you mean when you said that life would present more painful circumstances than the physical injury caused by accident, but I could never have imagined that *you* would be the source of my pain, Papa." Sobbing, Arielle stood, took her crutches, and left the room, leaving Daniel sitting there, his gaze fixed, with the dried solitary rose in his hand.

Chapter 23

Flashbacks

"What's wrong, Liebchen?[16]" Hans's mother asked when he returned home.

"Mutti,[17] the past twelve hours have been the worst in my life." Hans sank down into a chair in the kitchen.

His mother, a woman in her late forties with blonde girls cascading to her shoulders and a kind, tender smile, took him in her arms. "What could be so bad in the life of a boy your age?" she asked.

"Well, I went to visit Arielle, the beautiful girl I told you about—the one I accidently hit with the car."

"How is she?" Hans's mother wanted to know.

"She is recovering, but something very strange happened," Hans began. "I gave her your book *Buch der Lieder*, with the rose inserted in the page containing "Allnächtlich im Traume" by Heine. She was so happy with the gift, but when her father picked it up and saw the rose, he became as white as a ghost. Then, suddenly, he became very angry with me—so angry that he could barely look at me—and he forbade his daughter from ever seeing me

---

[16] A term of endearment, akin to "my love."

[17] Mom.

again. I don't know what I've done, Mutti. I was just trying to get to know this girl. She is very special."

Hans observed that his mother was troubled. "Do ... you know ... the ... father's name?" she stammered.

"Daniel Bouchard," Hans replied, wondering what could be wrong.

"Oh," was the only syllable that his mother managed to utter.

"Mutti, are you all right?" Hans asked, placing a hand on his mother's shoulder, observing her turning slightly pale.

"I will be. Please don't worry. I just have to run upstairs to make a telephone call. Oh, by the way, do you have Mr. Bouchard's phone number?"

"Yes, here's his business card, and on the back, you will find his home number," Hans said, presenting the card.

Life was becoming stranger and stranger for young Hans, who was beginning to believe that he just had to accept whatever came his way and brace himself for more unusual events. As he sat for a moment to ponder, he heard the following one-sided conversation take place in his mother's room.

"Joshua, you won't believe it. I found Daniel. Will you come? I have to explain what happened ... Yes, that's right. You heard me correctly ... Well, it's a long story, but I feel that everything happens for a reason ... Absolutely ... So you will? ... Make the appointment. Don't say anything about me. Just set the tone so that it won't be a total shock. I know ... It will be enough of a huge surprise, but ... *I have to do this.* I know that you understand. You're a good friend. I'm so glad that we've been in touch for these last few years. You're a godsend ... Tomorrow? 3:30? ... That's fine. Thank you! Let me give you his contact information."

Reading from the business card, Greta presented Daniel's home and business numbers to Joshua, who took them down by hand.

A few minutes after this communication took place, the phone rang in Daniel's home. He was lying on the couch watching television, while the girls and Jean Pierre were in their rooms studying. Arielle was still traumatized and refused to speak with him.

"I'll get it!" Daniel said, adding inaudibly to himself, *As if anyone else will. I am on the outs with my children just now. I cannot blame them for being angry and bewildered. The past is coming back to haunt me somehow, and I cannot believe that this has happened. Because of my own fractured heart, I hurt the one I love most, my beloved daughter.*

140

"Hello?" Daniel interrupted his quiet thought ramblings to answer the phone.

"Daniel, do you know who this is?"

The voice sounded familiar. Daniel paused and reflected.

After a few seconds, the speaker declared, "It's Joshua from college!"

"Joshua? I cannot believe it! How are you, man?"

"Oh, you know … a little older and grayer." Joshua laughed. "How are you?"

"Fine, generally. The same as you. Oh my God! To what do I owe this surprise?"

"Well, I live in Chicago, but I'm in town for a week, and I want to see you to talk about old times and revisit the past a little. I have a concert at Lincoln Center in three days, and I hope that you can attend, but first, it would be great to catch up. Would three thirty tomorrow afternoon work?"

"As you know, the past is my least-favorite subject. So, you're still singing, huh? You have a great career, I imagine," Daniel changed the subject for a moment.

"Well, it's a living. An artist lives for the art itself. I regularly perform at the Chicago Opera Theater. I have a following," Joshua said with characteristic humility.

"I'm sure your audience appreciates you. Yes, come to my office tomorrow at three thirty. I'll clear some time. The address is 5555 Fifty-Seventh Street."

"That means a lot. Thanks, brother!"

"It will be great to see you, buddy!"

"By the way, how did you get my phone number?" Daniel questioned.

"Believe me, it was easy. I will tell you tomorrow."

When the two hung up the phone, Daniel breathed deeply, and his heart quickened. *Somehow, I've found the past again—or the past has found me. It must be for a purpose. Everything has meaning in this world. I have to relax my mind and not allow myself to wallow in what used to be. I'm a grown man, and I can handle things. I know that's what Pierre would tell me. Sooner or later, things catch up with every one of us. Joshua was always a good friend, and although he reminds me of the happiest—and saddest—time in my life, we are in a different space now, and I have to refrain from living the memories and concentrate on the here and now.*

With these thoughts in mind, Daniel went about his day, allowing Arielle to brood in private over her broken heart. Her father had interfered in a budding relationship that promised to be so joyful and meaningful.

It will blow over, and everything will be back to normal in no time. I only want her happiness, he told himself, never stopping to think how contradictory his feelings and actions had been.

The next day, he went to work and told his secretary to let Joshua in without introduction. In the meantime, he emailed the CEO, informing him that all was well, and he was ready to resume the meeting that had begun via video conferencing from Dubai.

Then, at the appointed hour, Joshua entered and found his friend with his head buried in a pile of spreadsheets, preparing for the next day's meeting. The two embraced and felt deeply moved to see one another after so many years.

"You look great, brother!" Joshua exclaimed. "You haven't changed."

"I think you need glasses, man, but thanks! I've been working a lot, and the stress sometimes gets to me," Daniel admitted.

"There's pressure in every job. Even working on my high Cs causes me to stress out." Joshua chuckled.

"I understand. Listen, I owe you an apology." Daniel lowered his head.

"For what?" Joshua was perplexed.

"All those years ago, I drifted from you, Carmen, and Sue. I was lovestruck, and I couldn't see very clearly. My emotions and focus were entirely concentrated on *her.*"

"All of us clearly observed that, and we just had to move on with our lives. It's all water under the bridge, you know, but I must tell you that for the past few years, I've been in touch with Greta."

Daniel swallowed hard. "Where is she?"

"She's here, in New York. She's happily married with two children, a son, and a daughter—lovely, well-mannered, intelligent children."

"How did you find her?" Daniel asked, still dignifiedly containing his emotions.

"You know, brother, there is a so-called social media platform now called Facebook where people can go online to connect with family and friends—even those they haven't seen or heard from for years."

"I've heard of that, but I just don't have the time or inclination—"

"Maybe you can check it out sometime. Anyway, I went online, and I was shocked to find her there. It was surreal." Joshua laughed again.

"Have you spoken to her?" Daniel asked.

"Of course, and I have also seen her on one occasion, and—"

"You know that she disappeared without a trace, without so much as a word of explanation."

"I now have the scoop on why that occurred," Joshua said. "She left to save your life, out of pure *selflessness*."

"If her motivations were so selfless, why didn't she communicate them to me directly?"

"Well, the situation was extremely delicate," Joshua explained. "When she left more than twenty years ago, she was protecting your very life. You see, her father was constantly under surveillance, suspected of affiliations with the Third Reich and World War II crimes against humanity. Consequently, *everyone* associated with him, including his family and others, were in imminent danger. If she had not left when she did and the way in which she did, your life would have been jeopardized. She told me she loved you too much to take that risk. At the time, she couldn't say a word to you because her phones were tapped, and she would have placed herself and her family in peril. Therefore, she had to negate any concerns for herself and own her life and surrender to circumstance, which meant going with her family, without any questions asked, back to Germany, where she lived under a cloud of suspicion, always moving from place to place. That's why she couldn't receive any correspondence whatsoever from anyone in or outside of her country. She expressed to me, quite sincerely, that she genuinely believed that somehow she would find a way to reach you, but as time passed and her letters went unanswered, she had no other choice but to move forward with her life. Sadly, four years after they left the United States, Greta's father passed away."

Suddenly, a soft knock interrupted their conversation.

"There's a lady here to see you," Joshua replied, rising to open the door, containing his inner anxiety.

In walked a woman in her midforties, crowned with soft blonde curls cascading to her shoulders. A strained expression marred her brilliant, perfect smile, and her eyes had lost some of their radiance, owing to life's struggles and tribulations. Otherwise, time had been kind to Greta, and deep within, she was the same person, with profound, though guarded, affections.

Upon seeing her, Daniel (who had been standing while speaking with Joshua) collapsed into his chair and turned to face a large office window behind him with his back to her. His mind raced and flooded with flashbacks—old memories, songs, images, and feelings. Then, turning slightly, he glared at Joshua.

"You knew about this, and you arranged this meeting without consulting me. I thought that you were a man of discernment and loyalty, and now you unleash this surprise on me, catching me completely off guard. I never knew that you were a game-player." Daniel's voice escalated.

"Don't be unreasonable, man. This had to happen. I know that you were wondering—pining—for years on end. The only way to move forward is to face the truth—the facts that will finally put an end to all of your speculation and doubt," Joshua replied, maintaining his composure.

"Daniel, if you would only hear me out," Greta ventured in a soft tone.

"You can stand there, holding the reigns, still controlling my emotions as you always have." Daniel swung his chair around to face Greta, his face crimson with anger and embarrassment. "Don't you know that everything I did in my life after you—every wrong decision, every mistake—was because of your callousness and lack of compassion? Your failure of communication has had a direct effect on virtually everyone I have ever loved since, and I have had to answer to those individuals—and myself—as a result. I have carried around a ten-ton weight on my shoulders, wondering what I could have done wrong, always trying to compensate for something that was not quite right in my life. Because of your silence, *everything*—no matter what the situation was—turned out (in my own mind) to be my fault, and I could never figure out why. But now I know. All that went wrong in my life (most of my decisions for which I now bear full responsibility) were made because there was a vacancy in my heart—a gaping hole that no one and nothing could fill ... because of *you*. You didn't have the decency to offer any explanation for your departure, much less answer my final letter that poured out the contents of my heart—"

"Your letter?" Greta interrupted, allowing her tears to fall. "I never received any letters from you at all. I wrote to you countless times without a response. I want to tell you that without knowing the full story, your accusations and blame are baseless and unfair. If you would only listen to me now ..."

With an air of understanding and empathy, Daniel rose and stepped forward to take Greta's hand. "I wrote to you all the time, and I never understood your silence—until Joshua just told me all that happened to you and your father. He told me about your father's passing. I'm so sorry." Daniel paused. "How is your mother?"

"She's holding strong, but she misses Father very much. At least now, she is taking joy in her grandchildren," Greta looked somber.

"I imagine so." "You know, I came looking for you."

"What? You were in Germany?" Greta asked in disbelief.

"Yes, in 1990, right after the collapse of the Berlin Wall."

Joshua gasped. "You really risked yourself. Where was your head?"

"Not attached to my shoulders, that's for sure. I was lucky to get out of there alive!"

Daniel proceeded to tell the entire tale of his impromptu trip to Germany and how he wore a journalist's badge and nearly encountered death amid a barrage of bullets. Greta and Joshua could hardly believe their ears.

"By that time, we had left the country and were in hiding," Greta explained. "My father's health was declining, and my mother could not bear to live in Frankfurter Allee any longer. So we left the country and went to Belgium, where I met my husband."

"And now, are you happy?" At that moment, Daniel felt a pervasive sense of peace descend upon him. At last, the truth was unfolding.

"After my initial depression over losing you, I resigned myself to the fact that I had to surrender to circumstance. After living for about six months in Belgium (more than twenty years ago now—it's hard to believe), I met someone who helped me through the pain of all that I had experienced. When he asked me to marry him, I didn't hesitate for a minute. He's a wonderful man, and we have two children—Hans and Kristina, sixteen and fifteen years of age."

"I'm so happy for you. Hans is a great kid. He told you about me, didn't he?" Daniel's demeanor softened by the minute.

"Yes, when he came home yesterday and told me about what happened and his gift of the book ... and the rose ..." Greta's voice trailed off, as she allowed her emotions to surface. "That's when I called Joshua to come here with me … to cushion the shock."

A long pause ensued, while Joshua stood by and observed his friends' interaction, quietly relieved that at last, a sense of finality had come to the two long-suffering hearts.

"I was thinking." Greta broke the silence. "What happened between us—all of the circumstances beyond our control—should not, in any way, determine our children's fate. Hans genuinely likes and admires Arielle."

"The feeling is entirely mutual." Daniel smiled graciously.

"Then allow destiny to carry them where it will, without our interference," Greta added.

"Please let your son know that he is welcome in our home at any time. Our door is always open. I just have one request: next time, please tell him to bring another book."

Both of them laughed. Greta look poignantly at Daniel. "You know, it was fate. If Hans had not brought that precise book to your daughter, we would never have been able to achieve a resolution to our past suffering."

"I agree entirely," Daniel said, placing a gentle hand on Greta's shoulder.

She looked at the time. "Well, I really had better be going, but I want you to know how much this meeting has meant to me," she said. "It was a kind of purification."

"I feel the same. And we have this rogue to thank!" Daniel remarked, as he hugged Joshua and slapped him on the back. "He is the ficklest dude in the world. Where do his loyalties lie? Conspirator! He didn't even consult his good buddy about one of the most incredible surprises of his life!" Daniel laughed good-naturedly.

"Do you honestly think that Greta could have pulled this off if I had breathed a single word to you? You would have protested to high heaven. A little shock value was in order here—all for your benefit, good man," Joshua said with an air of self-satisfaction.

"Of course you're right. I would never have consented to this meeting, and I would never have wanted to reencounter the past, but now I realize that doing so has helped me to put things in perspective, and a tremendous weight has been lifted from my shoulders."

"I could not be happier!" Greta said as she embraced Daniel, who felt that this gesture was life-giving, sadly coming twenty years too late.

"Why couldn't you have given me this hug before entering the terminal twenty years ago?" he asked, half laughing.

Greta smiled as tears filled her eyes. "It's better late than never," she said.

Soon, Joshua said his goodbyes as well, making his friend promise that they would attend his concert in a few days.

"It wouldn't miss it, brother," Daniel assured him.

Then, as Joshua left and Daniel settled back into his office chair again, he suddenly felt free. As he closed his eyes and breathed a sigh of relief, the phone rang. It was his company's CEO.

"We are so glad that your daughter is recovering well, and we look forward to seeing you tomorrow. I'm just calling to confirm."

"Thank you! I'll be there at nine o'clock sharp," Daniel said decisively. He sensed that something new and promising was about to happen … and he was right.

Upon entering his office the next morning, the CEO and several staffers greeted him warmly before immersing themselves in conversation. "Daniel, your expertise is still needed in Dubai. We are still in financial quicksand, and your intervention will, no doubt, assist in extricating us from the economic quagmires in which we find ourselves. Management is failing, and your presence there is vital."

"Of course, I will be glad to implement the plans that we have discussed and report back to you." Daniel was pleasantly surprised by this news. Returning to the UAE would afford him the time and opportunity to slow down a little and focus on his work, and one thing was certain: he would never allow himself to brood or pine for love again. For the first time in his life, his heart was open … or so he thought.

Chapter 24

A Blank Slate

For the first time in his life, Daniel felt that he had attained inner harmony. As the chapter on his past relationship with Greta closed, a whole world of prospects seemed to open—not to mention his own heart, which was now a blank slate upon which a new life story could be written, free of regrets.

With this understanding, he flew to Dubai, asking Georgette to remain on hand for the children. This time, she didn't have to travel to their side, as they were old enough to care for themselves. However, all they had to do was say the word, and she would be there.

When he arrived at his corporate apartment, Daniel immersed himself in work, as he endeavored to deal with his company's financial quagmire. During a break, he allowed his thoughts to take flight and roam in a million directions.

I must call Jong-Hyun to try and establish contact with Annabelle, the daughter whom I have never met in Korea. A biological father has every right to see his child, and she has the same entitlement to know him. Such a connection must not be restrained or kept secret.

With these notions in view, he picked up the phone and called Jong-Hyun. "Doctor, it's Daniel. Please don't hang up. I'm fully aware that Mi Jin does not wish to hear from me at all and that she has no desire for our daughter to establish a relationship with me. However, I have concluded that she is not acting in Annabelle's best interests."

"What do you mean by this, and how can you purport to know what's good for the girl when you have never been in her life?" Jong-Hyun said firmly.

"Sir, please understand me. I deeply respect and admire you and Mi Jin and her right to privacy. However, I am also very aware that in most modern, progressive societies, the biological parent's legal rights are paramount. Besides, I have a moral responsibility to follow through on my obligations to the child as her father, as well as an undeniable emotional connection to her. She should know her brother and sisters and me, and we should be allowed to join together, as a family, without any interference."

"You make a compelling case, but you should have thought of this when you left my niece without any explanation for your silence," the protective uncle replied.

"I stand corrected, and I am more than cognizant of my failure to communicate. I can do nothing more at this point than sincerely apologize and try to move forward honorably and with love for my daughter." Daniel stood his ground. "You know, I essentially grew up without my parents due to tragic circumstances. I would have given anything for even one more moment with them. My mother died when I was three, and my father, who meant the world to me, was killed in a car accident when I was twelve. Several years later, my beloved grandmother met the same fate, but Annabelle and I have a chance to get to know one another, and I will not relinquish that sacred bond—*ever!*"

"I'm so sorry to hear of your terrible loses, and in my heart, I know that you are genuine. I understand your position, and I will speak to my niece within the next few days and get back to you," Jong-Hyun promised.

"I would greatly appreciate that." Daniel breathed a sigh of relief.

Three days elapsed, and when no word came, Daniel began to worry. Then, just as he was about to call Jong-Hyun with an even stronger demand, the phone rang. It was a Sunday, and Daniel was relaxing in his apartment.

"I spoke with Mi Jin, and she has agreed to allow you to talk with Annabelle. They will await your call," the physician said decisively, providing the appropriate country code and phone number.

"Thank you for making our communication possible, which means more to me than I can express. At last, I will know my daughter and be able to pour out my love and commitment to her, from the depths of my heart," Daniel affirmed.

"You are very welcome. I know that you are emotionally invested and will do right by my girls," Jong-Hyun answered.

After this pleasant conversation came to an end, the floodgates opened, and Daniel allowed himself to sob. As scenes from many segments of his life flashed before his eyes, he leaned into the pain and relived various emotions. This proved to be an incredibly cathartic exercise, and he braced himself for his next step.

How will she react when she hears my voice? Does she even know that I exist? If not, will she feel comfortable speaking with a stranger?

Daniel's hands trembled slightly as he dialed the number. "Hello, Mi Jin? It's me, Daniel."

"Oooooh! I am so happy! I have waited for you to call. I'm sorry. At first, I didn't know what to do, but then my uncle told me how much you wanted to make a connection to Annabelle—our daughter." As she spoke, Mi Jin's voice shook a little. She was overwhelmed.

"Please, you mustn't apologize! It is I who owe you a huge explanation. My work took me from everything and everyone, but I never forgot you, and I had every intention of calling and returning to you," Daniel began.

"Let's leave the past where it belongs—in the past. Right now, there is someone who will be pleased to speak with you," Mi Jin offered, graciously avoiding an uncomfortable topic. "Annabelle!" she called loudly.

"Wait!" Daniel cried. "How will she understand me? I don't speak a word of Korean."

"I named her Annabelle, which I chose because of the story that you told me about the nurse who saved your daughter, Arielle. Over the years, I made sure that she learned English, in hopes that one day you would find and recognize her as your own," Mi Jin explained.

"Come, there is someone who is interested in speaking with you, darling!"

Daniel was near tears when Annabelle came to the phone. "Hello, Annabelle. My name is Daniel. I am your dad!" The words came out of his mouth as naturally as his name.

"Hi!" came the soft, sweet voice of the ten-year-old girl. "I am happy to meet you."

Daniel was astonished by her command of the English language.

"I would love to see you in person someday, hold you in my arms, and never let go," Daniel said through his tears.

"I would love that too! Maybe, I can come to America and visit you, or you can travel here," Annabelle suggested.

"You can count on it, my love. I will be there as soon as I can," Daniel assured his daughter.

Now, my life is complete— except for the fact that I need someone to share it with, someone with whom I can laugh, cry, plan for the future, and honestly be myself, Daniel told himself. Suddenly inspired, he decided to go outside and paint the sunset. It was dusk, and he was alone but no longer lonely. Looking down, he admired the blank canvas and all the possibilities it held.

Chapter 25

A Second Chance, a Second Rose

After several days' more work, Daniel's friend Ahmed invited him to a golfing club. "All of the US and French presidents' favorite pastime is golfing. Why should you shy away from it?" Ahmed teased.

"You're right. I could use a couple of days off. Count me in," Daniel replied.

He packed his bags and headed out. When he arrived at his destination, he called his children via cellphone. He loved the new technology and spent more time checking in and making sure that his family was doing well. Claudette joked that her father had a new part of his anatomy called an iPhone growing out of his ear.

Ahmed and Monique, his wife, were delighted that Daniel was willing to engage in recreation, because he was always buried in his work, ostensibly averse to socialization. "It's time to open your heart, my friend," Ahmed declared.

"Consider it done. I don't have any restrictions now. I am a free man—emotionally and psychologically—and I'm ready to move forward with my life," Daniel assured him.

Hearing these words prompted Ahmed to devise his long-awaited matchmaking plan. "We'll invite Daniel to the luncheon at the club tomorrow. I want him to meet Mariana. I think they would be perfect together."

"You have a sense of such things, and I trust your judgment. Mariana will be captivated by his charm and good nature. She is very special and deserves the very best. I don't want her to get hurt. She is a rare flower—a beauty inside and out."

"Don't worry, darling. I hardly recognize Daniel. All of his innate genuine qualities are resurfacing. He is no longer guarded and restrained. He seems to be cured of lovesickness," Ahmed observed.

"I trust you, and I will pray that the arrangement works out," Monique said.

The next day, the couple invited their friend to a luncheon, at which he met with a lovely young woman. Her shy, cautious demeanor appealed to him. She was devoid of ego and wore a benevolent expression. Her intelligent eyes seemed to be the windows to Daniel's soul, and she found everything he said to be amusing.

With one request from Daniel, "Tell me about yourself," the conversation lasted for more than three hours, and both Mariana and he felt as though they had known each other forever.

"Let's meet tomorrow without our friends. Don't get me wrong, I love them, but I want to steal you away." Daniel's charisma was undeniable.

"Why do you assume that I want to be stolen?" Mariana asked demurely.

Daniel laughed. "I can tell by the look in your eyes," he replied. "Meet me tomorrow at the local electronics store. I have to purchase a new laptop. I'm running out of RAM."

"Is that your idea of a romantic date, and what is RAM anyway?" Mariana queried, giggling.

"RAM is a computer's random-access memory, which affects a user's ability to perform tasks simultaneously and optimize the system's performance."

"I still don't know what you're talking about." Mariana laughed.

"Well, let's put it this way: as far as we are concerned, RAM means 'romance always matters.'"

"You really *are* a charmer."

Daniel blushed and took his leave. "I'll see you tomorrow."

The next day, as Daniel was searching for the right laptop at the electronics store, a young woman came up to him holding a red rose. Stunned, he turned to look at her. Mariana tenderly returned his glance.

"Is that for me?" Daniel asked.

"Yes, of course. I know that you are seeking RAM—a romance that always matters, and this is the start of something beautiful," Mariana replied, mustering her courage to speak candidly.

At that moment, he realized that he had encountered his second—and final—rose, one that would complete him and make his life meaningful. No longer did he fear abandonment, no longer did he want to strategize and scheme about how he would hold onto her. He just knew that she would be there for and with him, unconditionally and without judgment.

The two spoke that day as if they had known one another for years, broaching personal subjects. He told her that he had three children living in the United States, and she mentioned her daughter, named Kyla. Over the course of their meeting, no topic was off limits, and the conversation flowed freely. Both agreed that they shared the same dream: to travel the world, serve the underprivileged, and bring comfort to downtrodden, economically disenfranchised populations at home and abroad.

Their relationship quickly evolved, and everything was perfect ... except ... yes, there *was* a caveat: Daniel had been keeping a secret. For several months, he had been writing his memoirs, but he never mentioned that fact to anyone—not even to his daughters. At some level, he still harbored a tremendous fear of revealing his truth to others, including his new love. Would she understand and love him if she knew the whole truth?

The answer unfolded when the two vacationed in Bora Bora, a South Pacific Island west of Tahiti when he decided to take a leap of faith. "Darling, there is something that I have meant to tell you."

"Anything. You know that you can confide in me."

"I have been writing my autobiography. It's all about a past that I am less than proud to claim as mine. I want you to read the draft manuscript so that you can decide our future as a couple."

"I don't have to read one word of what you have written. I accept you as you are. Contingencies and barriers do not exist in our relationship. You deserve every happiness, including the publication of your book, and I will support you in that goal."

Daniel was overwhelmed with joy. Six months later, he proposed, and the couple was married in a small ceremony surrounded by close friends and family members. Ahmed and Monique, the glowing matchmakers, proudly stood among the company, which consisted of Mariana's sister as the maid of honor; bridesmaids Arielle and Claudette; best man Jean Pierre (having just turned fifteen); and the bride's daughter, Kyla, as the flower girl. Pierre, Adelle, and family were also in attendance, as were Daniel's sisters, Colette and Marie, all embodying the ever-present spirits of Papa and Grand-mère.

Rays of golden light, mixed with various hues of the spectrum, shone like prisms over the couple, signifying that the heavenly guests were, in fact, there to celebrate their union.

Instead of a honeymoon, the couple decided that they would fulfill their most heartfelt aspiration of traveling to the neediest countries. "But first, we have something very important to do," Daniel announced.

"What is that? I'm ready if you are!" Mariana said lightheartedly, always ready for adventure.

"We must visit my daughter in Seoul, South Korea."

"I didn't know …" Mariana looked surprised.

"You didn't seize the chance to read my book and learn all the details of my past," Daniel teased.

"I am pleasantly intrigued," Mariana reassured him. "I will book a flight, and after you complete your ongoing company rescue project, we will go—together."

Life proceeded apace. Georgette remained in Paris and traveled at every opportunity to see her angels. She never remarried but felt utterly content with her life and family commitments, always jovial, optimistic, and focused.

Daniel and Georgette's three children quickly became model adults, close to both parents and always ready to assist them in every way possible. The girls studied law and became successful attorneys, with licenses in New York and Michigan. Jean Pierre followed in his father's footsteps and became his right arm in the business, and Annabelle ... well, she was still growing up, eager to see her father.

"When will you visit?" she asked. "I cannot wait to finally meet you in person."

"I'm planning on next week. I am dreaming of holding you in my arms and never letting go," Daniel replied with joyful tears in his eyes.

Soon, he and Mariana were at the airport, boarding their flight to Seoul. A flood of memories came pouring into Daniel's mind and heart. Somehow, airports triggered that sentiment all the time. Mariana encouraged him to speak his mind, and unlike in times past, he opened up as readily as the pages of a book, talking freely about everything in his life. At times, he paused and looked solemn, but his wife always knew how to evoke his smile—the ray of light from within.

He grew to acknowledge and admit his mistakes while refraining from self-chastisement and regret. "Past mistakes are building blocks for the future and precursors to happiness," he wrote in his manuscript. His epilogue follows, summarizing his message to himself and others.

Epilogue

Regret is a terrible word—and an even worse feeling to nurture. Therefore, let go and set yourself free. Valuable lessons are outgrowths of the pain of mistakes. Without them, you cannot be the partner, parent, sibling, son, daughter, or friend you wish to be. You cannot grow, evolve, or empathize with others, and you will not be able to fulfill your manifest destiny. As the English poet Alexander Pope (1688–1744) wrote in *An Essay on Criticism*, "To err is human, to forgive is divine." The key is to forgive yourself. Self-introspection is fine, but not when you find yourself continually second-guessing your thoughts, feelings, and actions, and you restrain your innate potential.

Commitment shouldn't hurt, and love should be natural—as painless as the rising and setting sun. Although pain is involved in the growth process, self-destructiveness is counterproductive. When you find someone with whom you can share your heart, seize the moment. Don't strangle the subject of your love. If that love has been ordained by providence, fate, or the divine (however you perceive the forces of life to be), it will endure. Allow life to proceed on its natural course, like a river that flows effortlessly on its path.

Devotion is synonymous with permanence. With regard to romantic relationships, hand-holding, embracing, and displays of affection must not be taken lightly. All are manifestations of binding loyalty. Don't play games, especially since signs of affection are definite indicators of a heart connection—not just fly-by-night encounters. Generally, women are especially in tune with such clues and are more inclined to respond to them and invest their hearts than men tend to be. Therefore, be careful and respectful of feelings and aware of the repercussions of your actions. Paying heed to consequences *before* becoming invested will avoid a lot of heartache and misunderstanding.

Make sure to be authentic with yourself and others. Hiding from the truth or the consequences that may ensue from your revelation only delays the inevitable. Face the music—the trauma of your past—no matter how difficult doing so may be, and dance through the struggle. In that instant, you will encounter yourself and your true purpose.

What others believe or think is irrelevant, for those who truly love you will accept you without any conditions or certainties. Life itself is filled with ambiguities, doubts, and inconsistencies, which must be embraced as lessons yet to be learned, and if you don't see a light at the end of the tunnel, light up the side where you stand. Others will notice!

Take it from me, Daniel Bouchard. I have emerged into the light, created by my own voice and commitment to the truth. Now, as I look back, I realize that there is so much more of my story to recount, but sometimes the memories are too painful to relive. Perhaps someday I will open my heart and allow myself to revisit some of the memories that I have omitted here. Over time, I have come to realize that none of us can erase the past. Instead, we can only ask for forgiveness. That, in itself, is the path to healing. I do so freely now. To all those whom I have mentioned, as well as to those I have not included in my narrative, I sincerely apologize for any errors or missteps that I may have committed. You know who you are, and you are in my thoughts. And to my readers, I am happy to have shared my story with you—with love, respect, and in solidarity.

CPSIA information can be obtained
at www.ICGtesting.com
Printed in the USA
FFHW02n2217050918
48186971-51912FF

9 781546 293651